Chillax!

How Ernie Learns to Chill Out, Relax, and Take Charge of His Anger

by Marcella Marino Craver, MSEd, CAS
illustrated by Amerigo Pinelli

Magination Press • Washington, DC
American Psychological Association

TO MIKE, MY ROCK, FOR YOUR LOVE AND OPTIMISM;
TO OUR GIRLS FOR THE INSPIRATION.
TO MOM AND DAD FOR PROVIDING THE FOUNDATION TO A
BEAUTIFUL LIFE. ALL OF YOU HAVE ENCOURAGED
ME TO DO WHAT I LOVE. — *MMC*

A MIO PADRE, PAOLO. — *AP*

Published by
MAGINATION PRESS
An Educational Publishing Foundation Book
American Psychological Association
750 First Street, NE
Washington, DC 20002

For more information about our books, including a complete catalog,
please write to us, call 1-800-374-2721, or visit our website
at www.apa.com/pubs/magination.

Book design by Sandra Kimbell

Printed by Worzalla, Stevens Point, WI

Library of Congress Cataloging-in-Publication Data

Craver, Marcella Marino.
Chillax! : how Ernie learns to chill out, relax, and take charge of his
anger / by Marcella Marino Craver ; illustrated by Amerigo Pinelli.
p. cm.
ISBN-13: 978-1-4338-1037-4 (pbk.)
ISBN-10: 1-4338-1037-9 (pbk.)
1. Anger in children--Juvenile literature. 2. Anger--Juvenile literature.
3. Graphic novels--Juvenile literature. I. Pinelli, Amerigo. II. Title.
BF723.A4C74 2012
155.1'1247--dc23
2011020624
Manufactured in the United States of America
10 9 8 7 6 5 4 3 2 1

Chillax!

Dear Reader

Anger can make life hard. If you're angry all the time, you might feel exhausted, and your out-of-control emotions can get in the way of your daily life and keep you from enjoying the activities and hobbies you like best. With some hard work, though, you can reduce your anger, which frees up your brain to think positive thoughts and gives you room to enjoy the day-to-day events in your life. Kids tend to be more successful in school once they get their anger under control. Life at home usually gets calmer and more predictable, and friendships grow deeper and more fulfilling.

By working hard, you can get your emotions under control and start feeling better. Here's how: First you must identify why and when you are angry and how you show that anger. From there, you can figure out how to decrease your anger and express it in more appropriate ways. *Chillax!* can help. It's a story about Ernie, who is learning to understand and control his anger. The kid-friendly resource section at the end of the book can provide you with even more tools and strategies for dealing with anger when it gets too big or out of control.

Many kids feel overwhelming anger. You are not alone. It will take dedication on your part to understand it and change your actions. Once you identify your physical signals of anger, you'll then be able to apply the SWIFT-B strategies to get in control of your reactions. While you're perfecting those, add activities to improve your overall emotional state—visualization, exercise, laughter, grateful journaling, and communication—to your day-to-day life. The effectiveness of each strategy and activity varies from person to person. Be persistent and find something that works for you. Good luck!

—Marcella

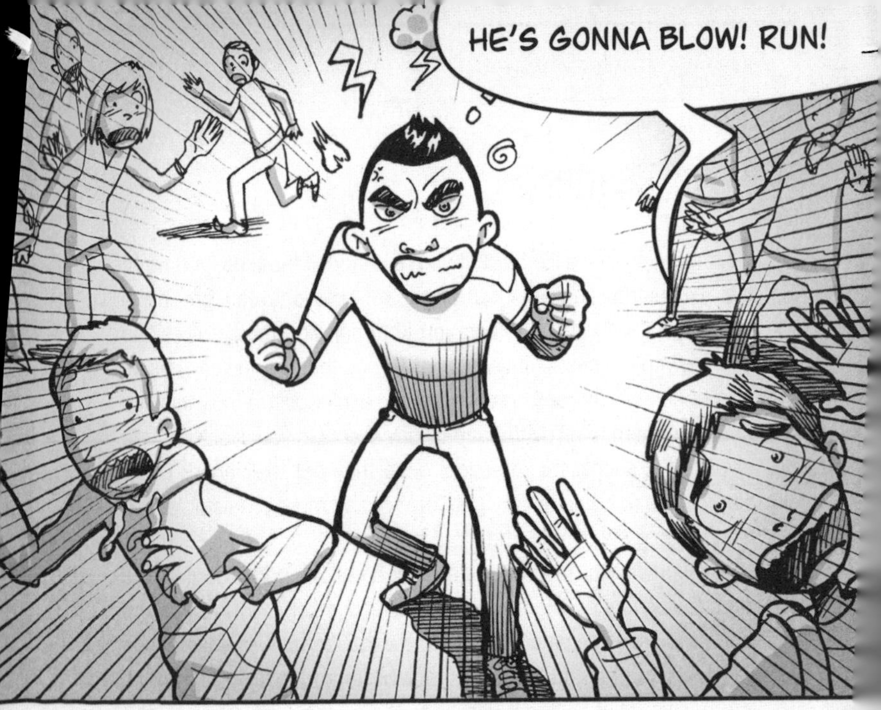
HE'S GONNA BLOW! RUN!

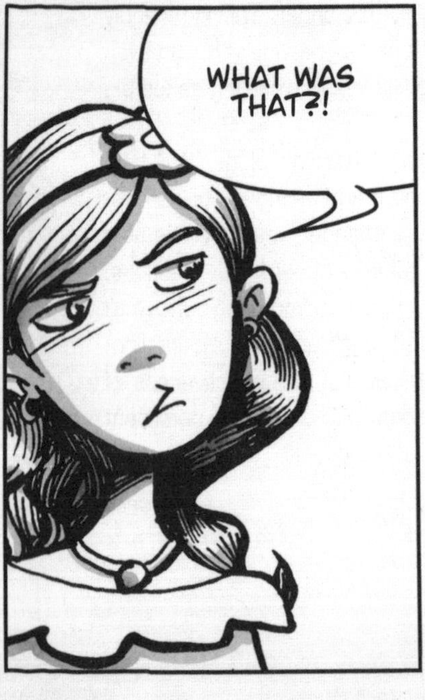
WHAT WAS THAT?!

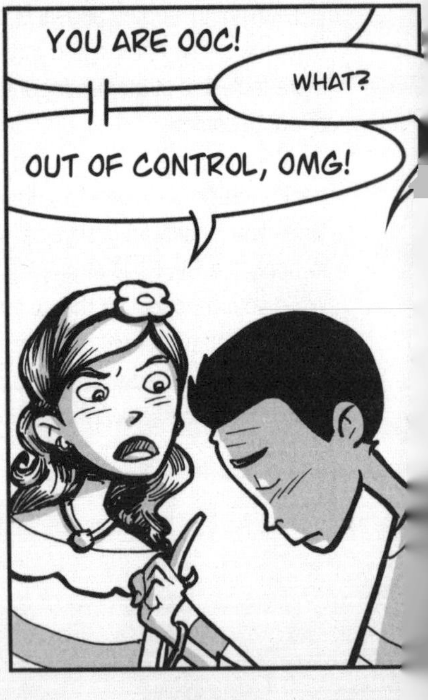
YOU ARE OOC!
WHAT?
OUT OF CONTROL, OMG!

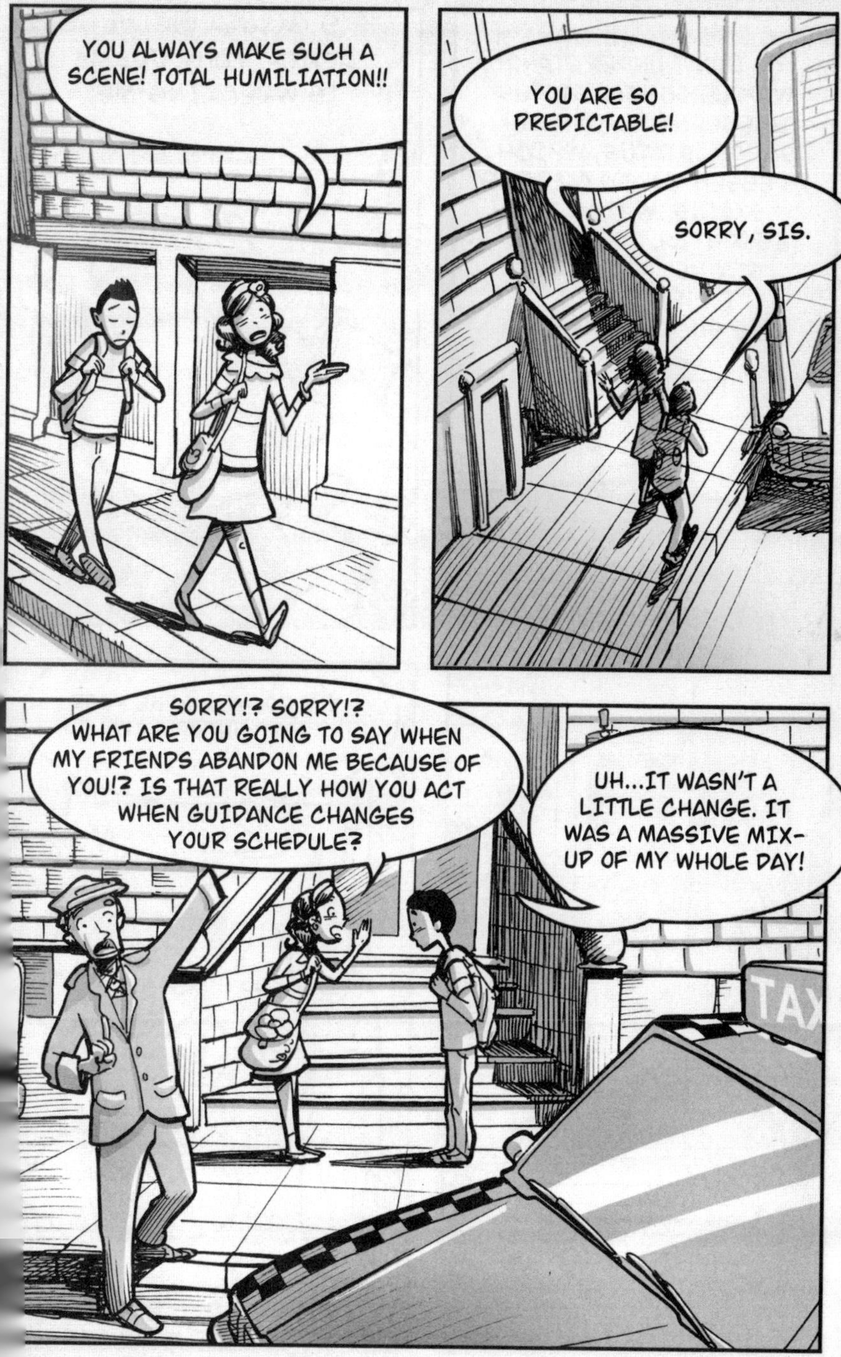

YOU ALWAYS MAKE SUCH A SCENE! TOTAL HUMILIATION!!
YOU ARE SO PREDICTABLE!
SORRY, SIS.
SORRY!? SORRY!? WHAT ARE YOU GOING TO SAY WHEN MY FRIENDS ABANDON ME BECAUSE OF YOU!? IS THAT REALLY HOW YOU ACT WHEN GUIDANCE CHANGES YOUR SCHEDULE?
UH...IT WASN'T A LITTLE CHANGE. IT WAS A MASSIVE MIX-UP OF MY WHOLE DAY!
TAX

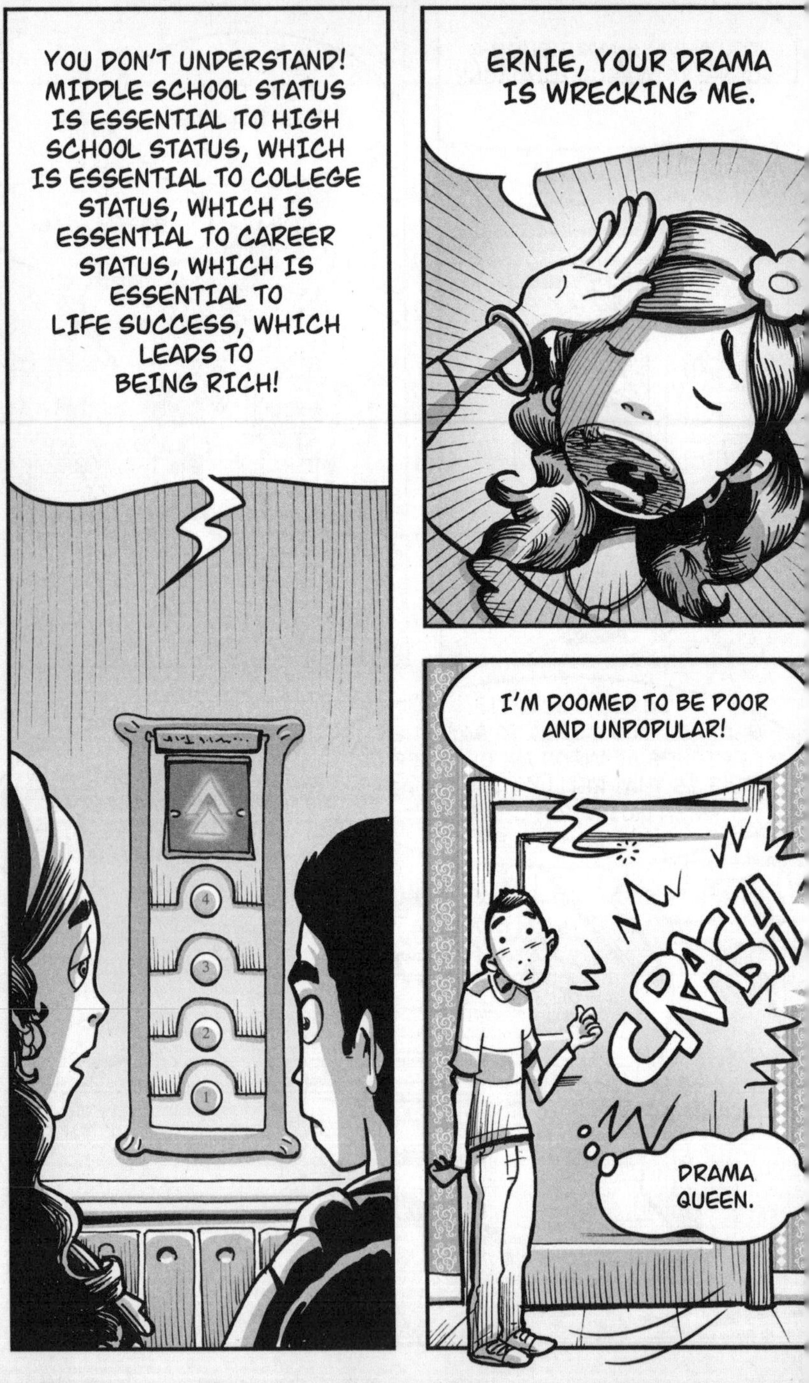
YOU DON'T UNDERSTAND! MIDDLE SCHOOL STATUS IS ESSENTIAL TO HIGH SCHOOL STATUS, WHICH IS ESSENTIAL TO COLLEGE STATUS, WHICH IS ESSENTIAL TO CAREER STATUS, WHICH IS ESSENTIAL TO LIFE SUCCESS, WHICH LEADS TO BEING RICH!
ERNIE, YOUR DRAMA IS WRECKING ME.
I'M DOOMED TO BE POOR AND UNPOPULAR!
CRASH
DRAMA QUEEN.

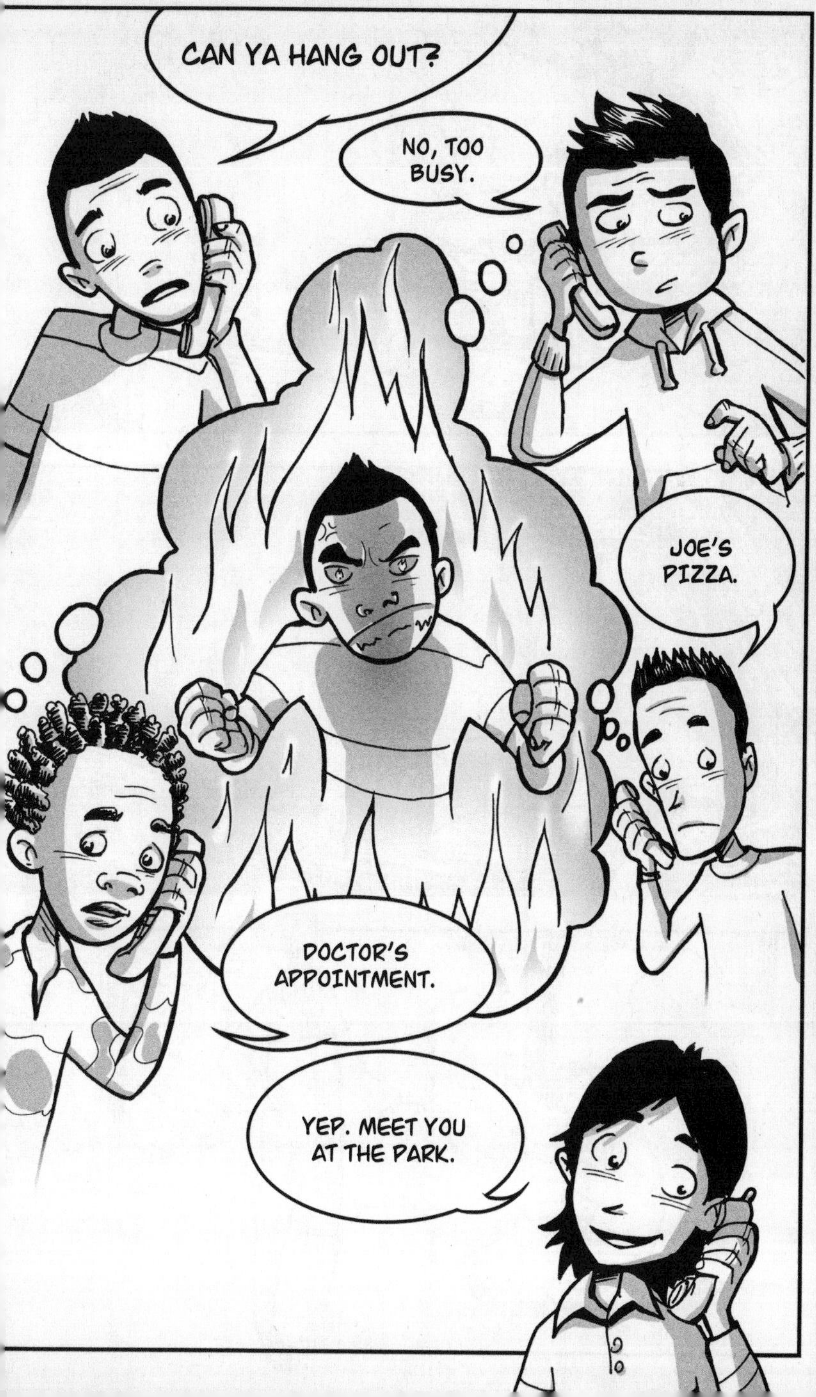
CAN YA HANG OUT?
NO, TOO BUSY.
JOE'S PIZZA.
DOCTOR'S APPOINTMENT.
YEP. MEET YOU AT THE PARK.

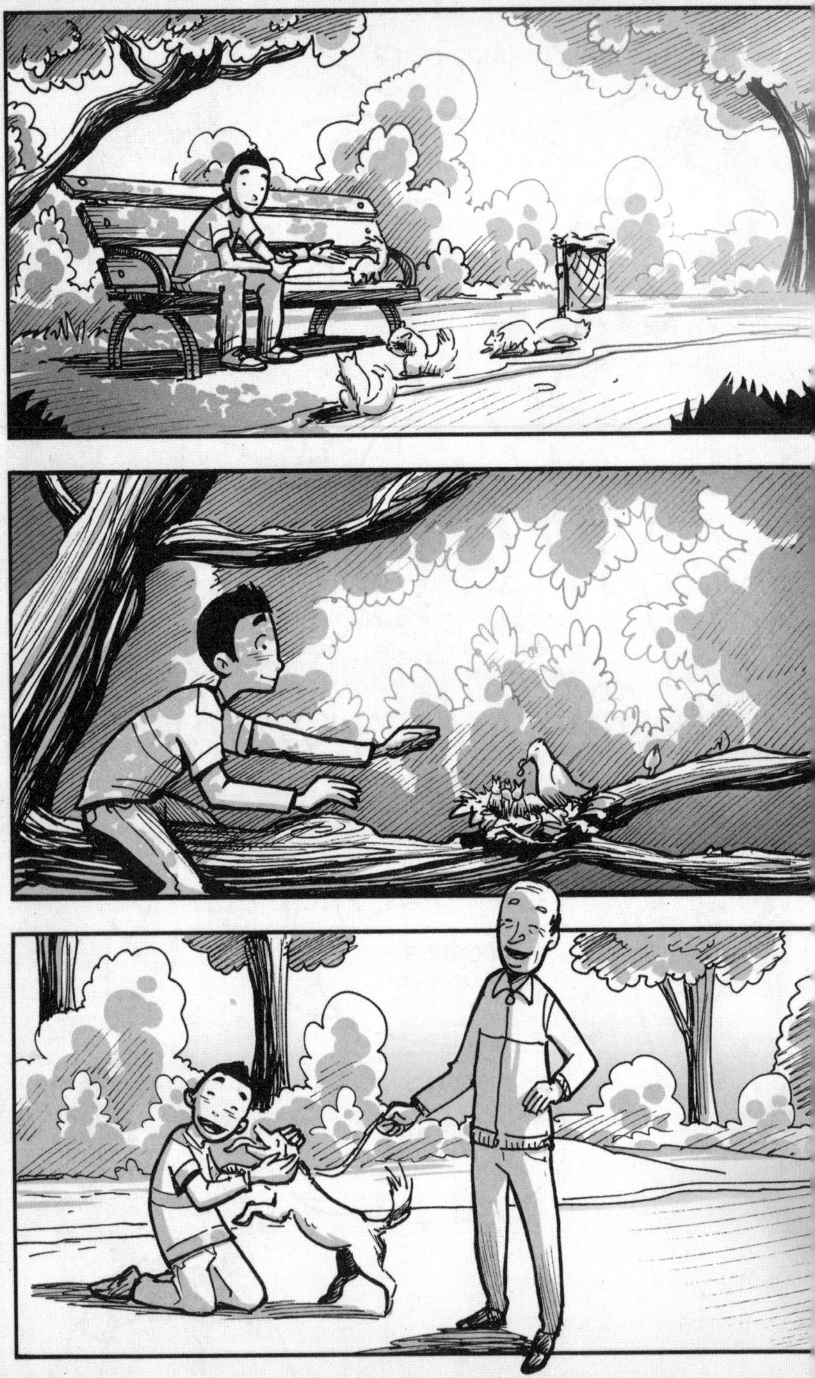

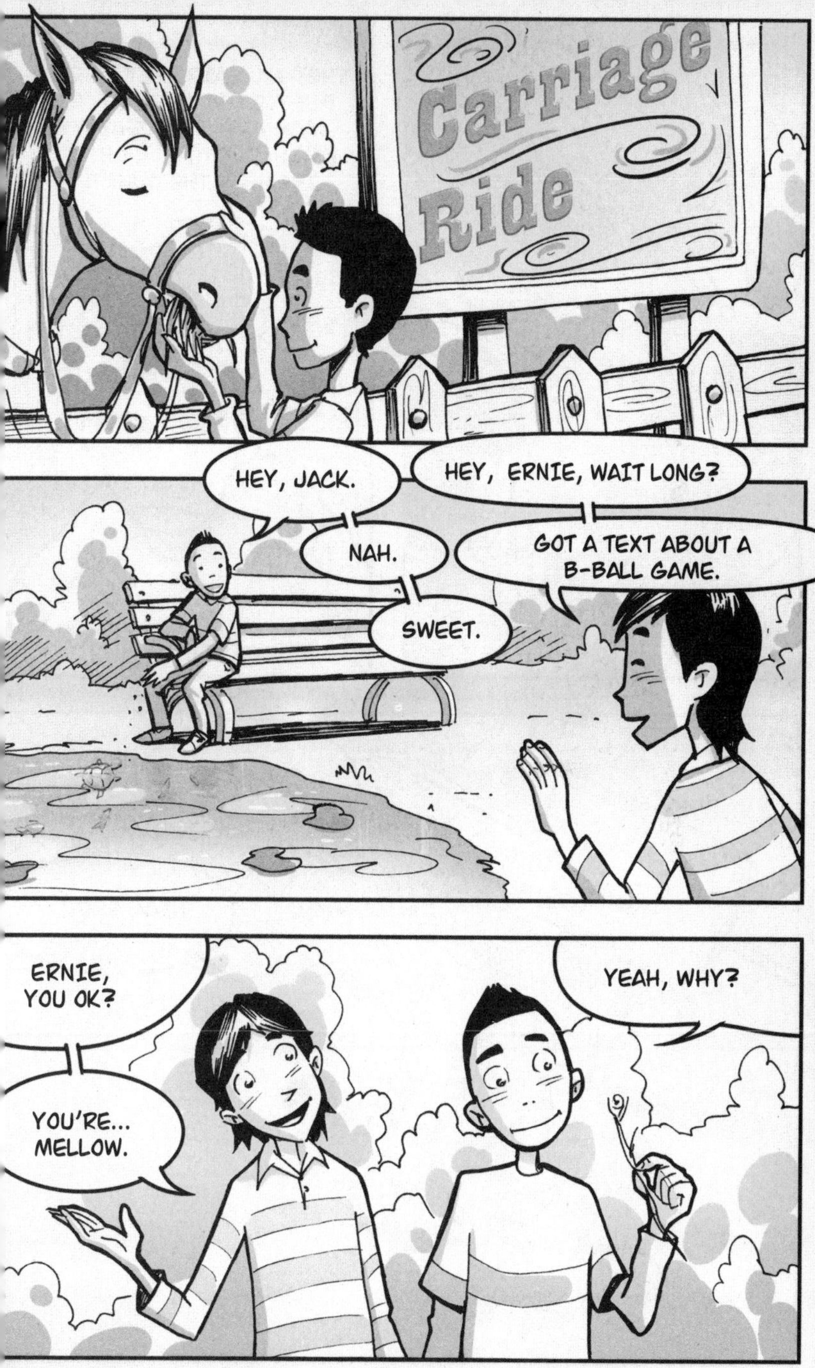
Carriage Ride
HEY, JACK.
HEY, ERNIE, WAIT LONG?
NAH.
GOT A TEXT ABOUT A B-BALL GAME.
SWEET.
ERNIE, YOU OK?
YEAH, WHY?
YOU'RE... MELLOW.

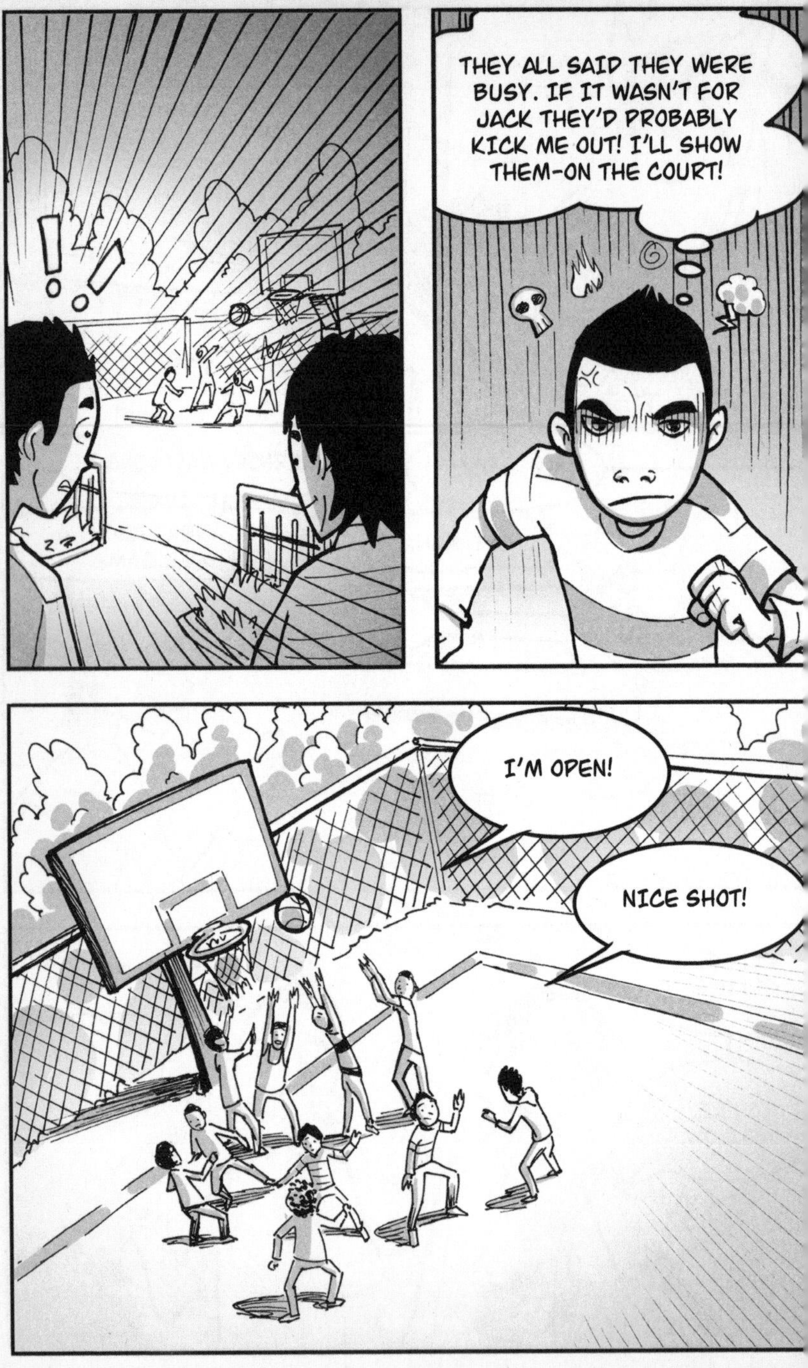

THEY ALL SAID THEY WERE BUSY. IF IT WASN'T FOR JACK THEY'D PROBABLY KICK ME OUT! I'LL SHOW THEM–ON THE COURT!
I'M OPEN!
NICE SHOT!

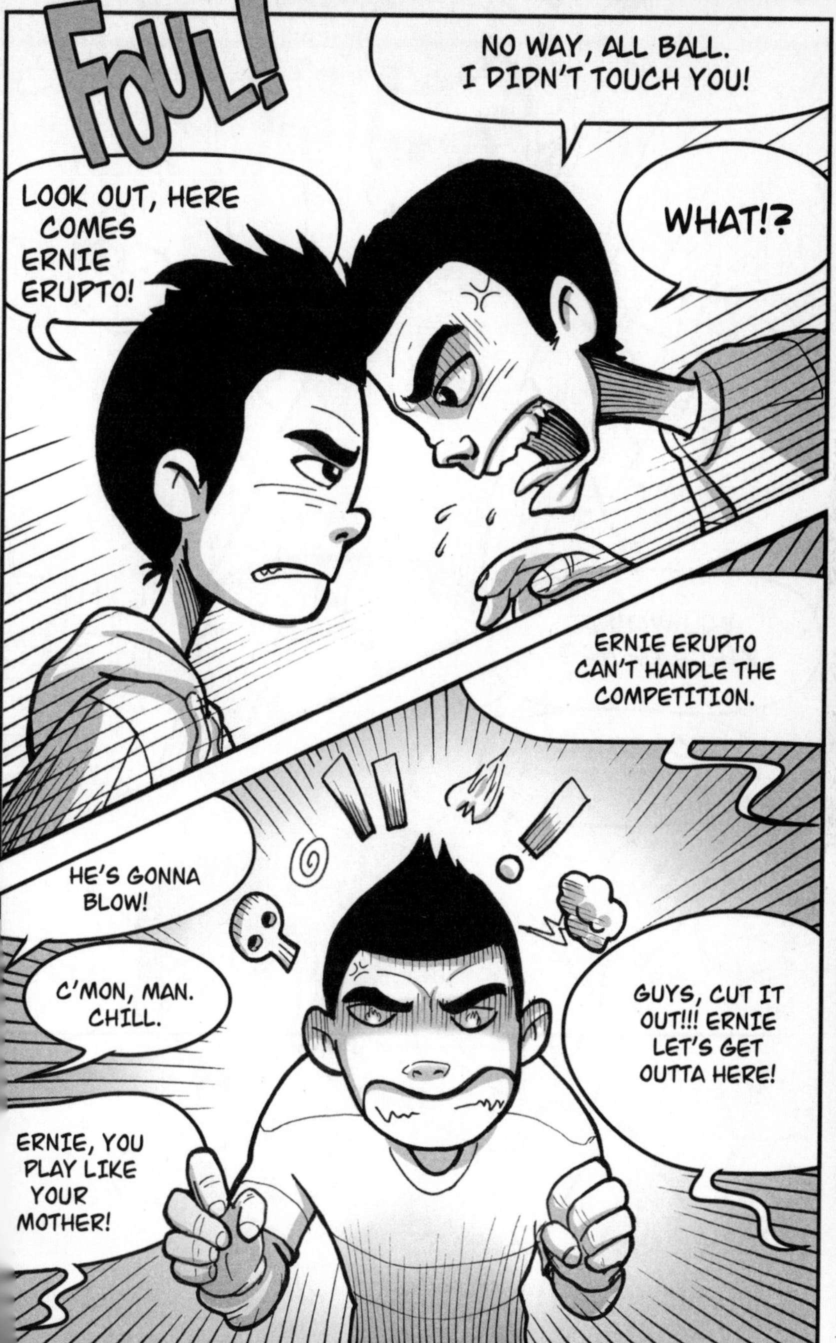
FOUL!
NO WAY, ALL BALL. I DIDN'T TOUCH YOU!
LOOK OUT, HERE COMES ERNIE ERUPTO!
WHAT!?
ERNIE ERUPTO CAN'T HANDLE THE COMPETITION.
HE'S GONNA BLOW!
C'MON, MAN. CHILL.
GUYS, CUT IT OUT!!! ERNIE LET'S GET OUTTA HERE!
ERNIE, YOU PLAY LIKE YOUR MOTHER!

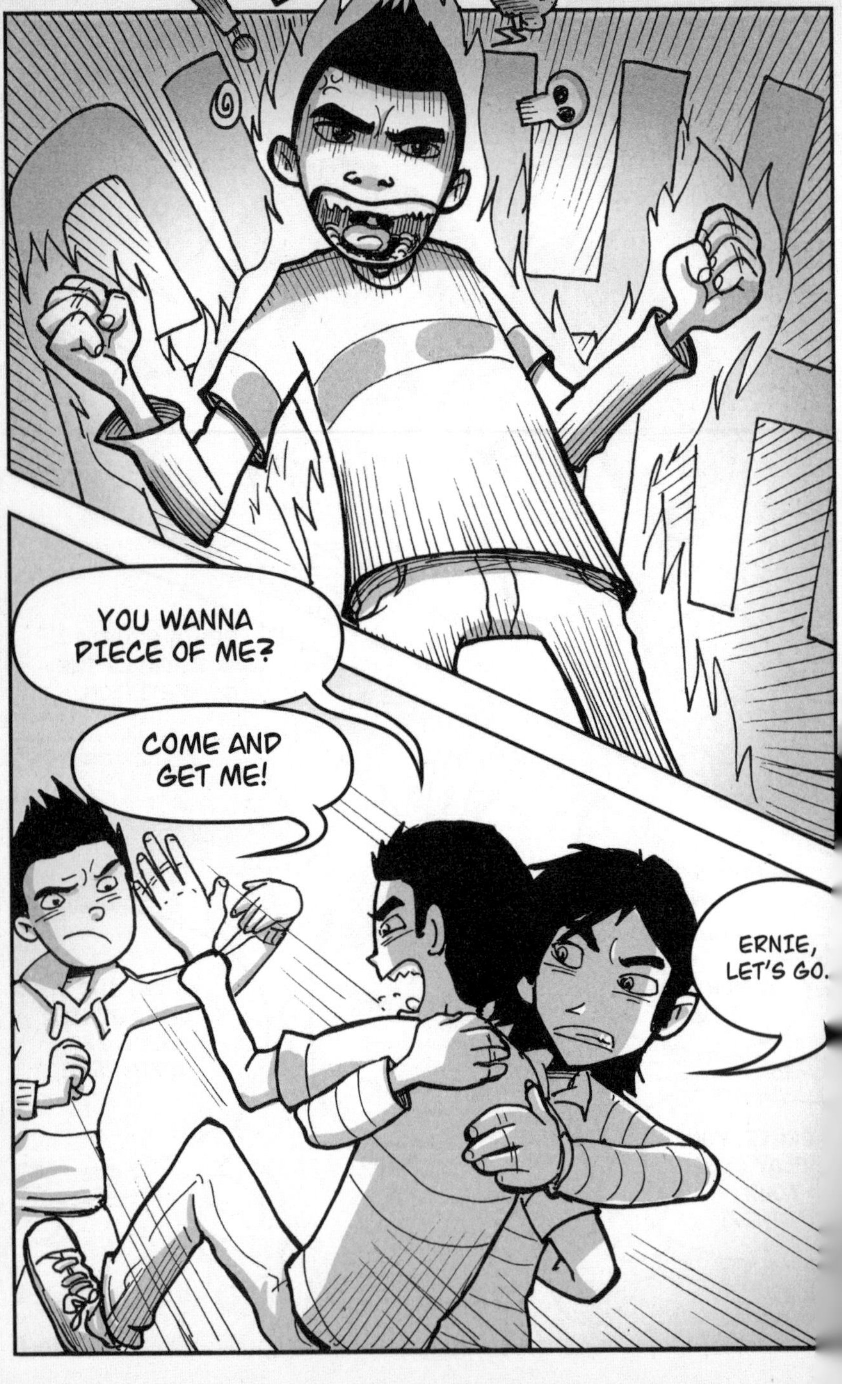
YOU WANNA PIECE OF ME?
COME AND GET ME!
ERNIE, LET'S GO.

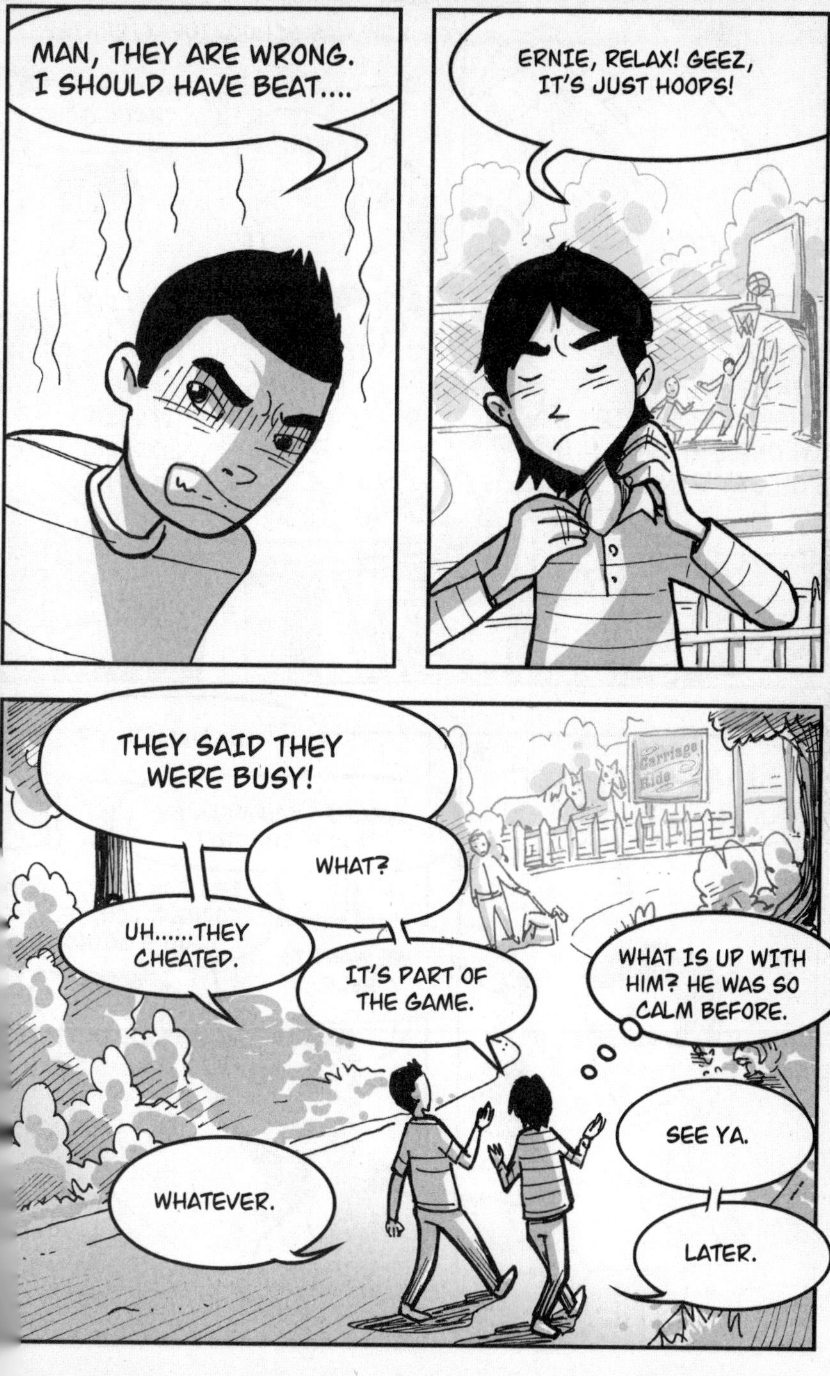
MAN, THEY ARE WRONG. I SHOULD HAVE BEAT....
ERNIE, RELAX! GEEZ, IT'S JUST HOOPS!
Carriage Ride
THEY SAID THEY WERE BUSY!
WHAT?
UH......THEY CHEATED.
IT'S PART OF THE GAME.
WHAT IS UP WITH HIM? HE WAS SO CALM BEFORE.
WHATEVER.
SEE YA.
LATER.

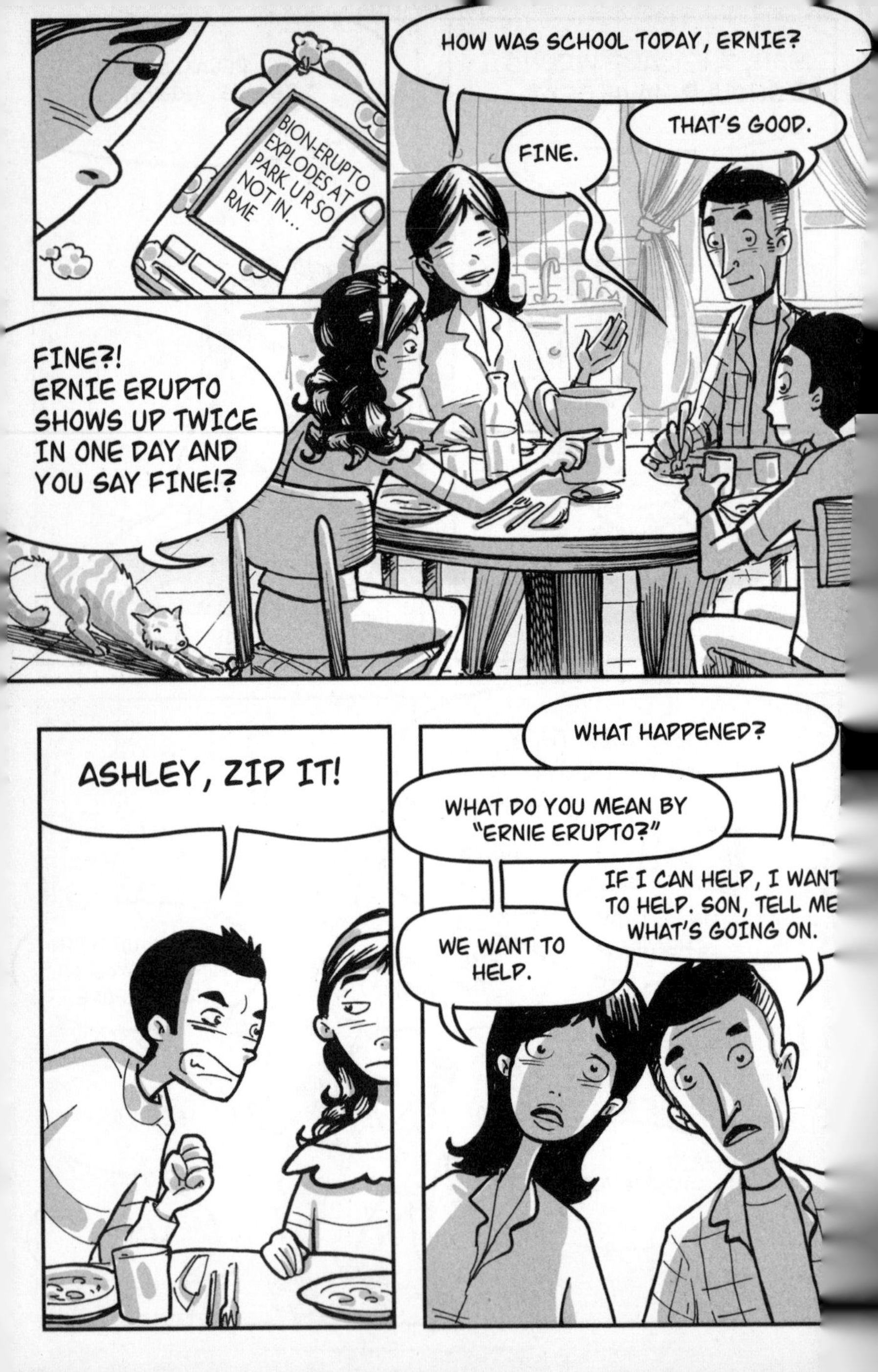
BION-ERUPTO EXPLODES AT PARK. U R SO NOT IN... RME
HOW WAS SCHOOL TODAY, ERNIE?
FINE.
THAT'S GOOD.
FINE?! ERNIE ERUPTO SHOWS UP TWICE IN ONE DAY AND YOU SAY FINE!?
ASHLEY, ZIP IT!
WHAT HAPPENED?
WHAT DO YOU MEAN BY "ERNIE ERUPTO?"
IF I CAN HELP, I WANT TO HELP. SON, TELL ME WHAT'S GOING ON.
WE WANT TO HELP.

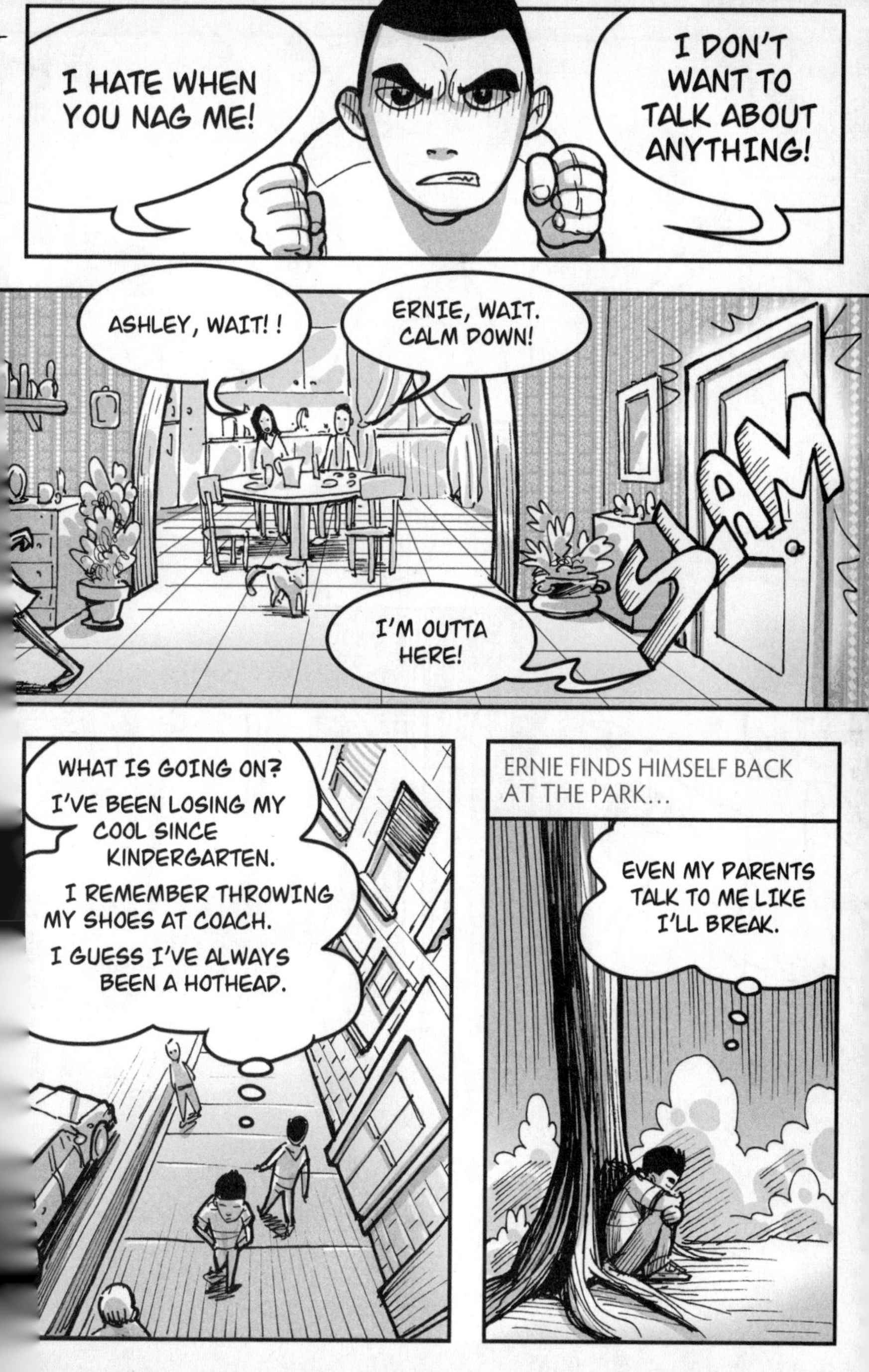
I HATE WHEN YOU NAG ME!
I DON'T WANT TO TALK ABOUT ANYTHING!
ASHLEY, WAIT! !
ERNIE, WAIT. CALM DOWN!
SLAM
I'M OUTTA HERE!
WHAT IS GOING ON?
I'VE BEEN LOSING MY COOL SINCE KINDERGARTEN.
I REMEMBER THROWING MY SHOES AT COACH.
I GUESS I'VE ALWAYS BEEN A HOTHEAD.
ERNIE FINDS HIMSELF BACK AT THE PARK…
EVEN MY PARENTS TALK TO ME LIKE I'LL BREAK.

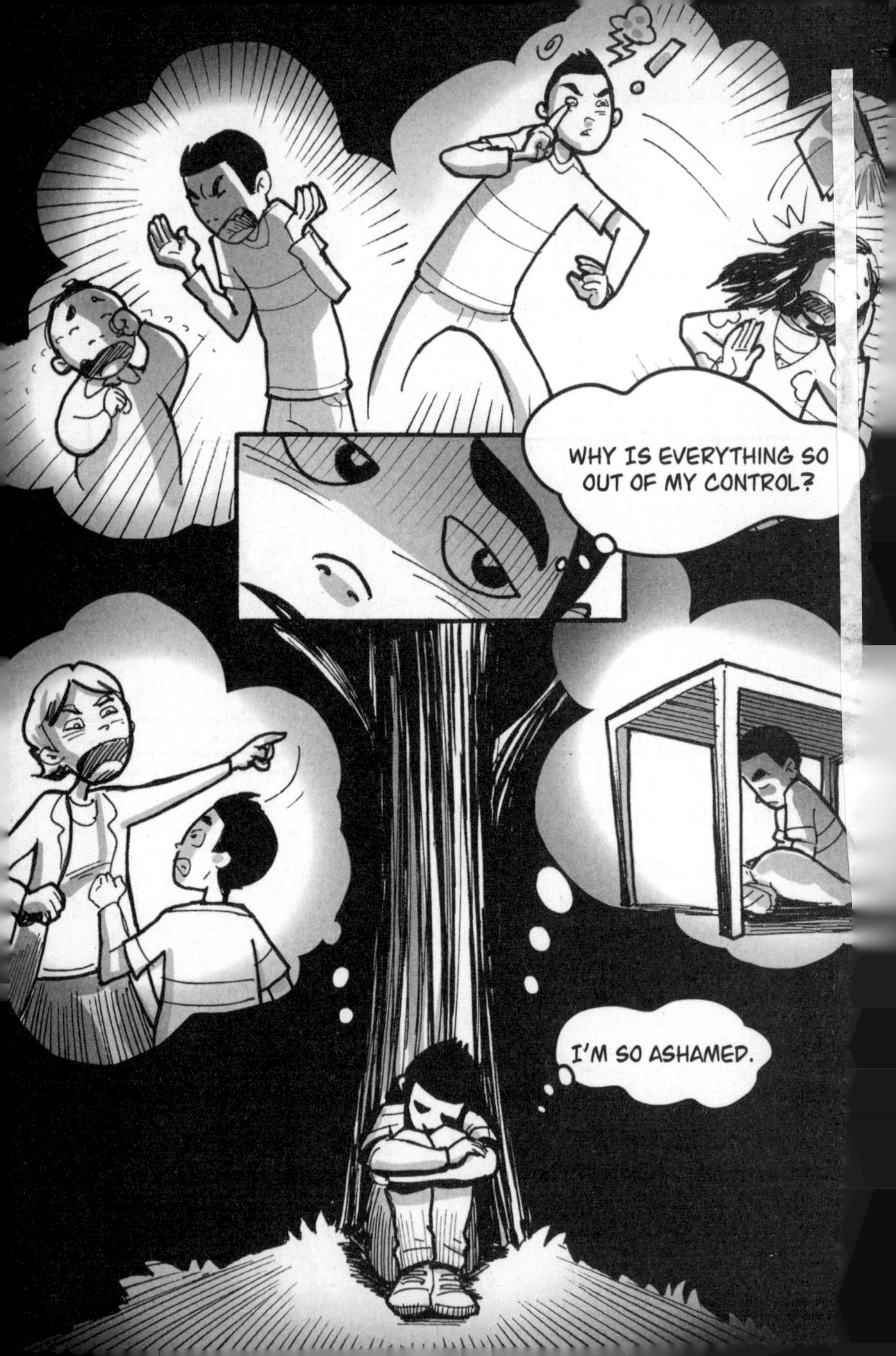
WHY IS EVERYTHING SO OUT OF MY CONTROL?
I'M SO ASHAMED.

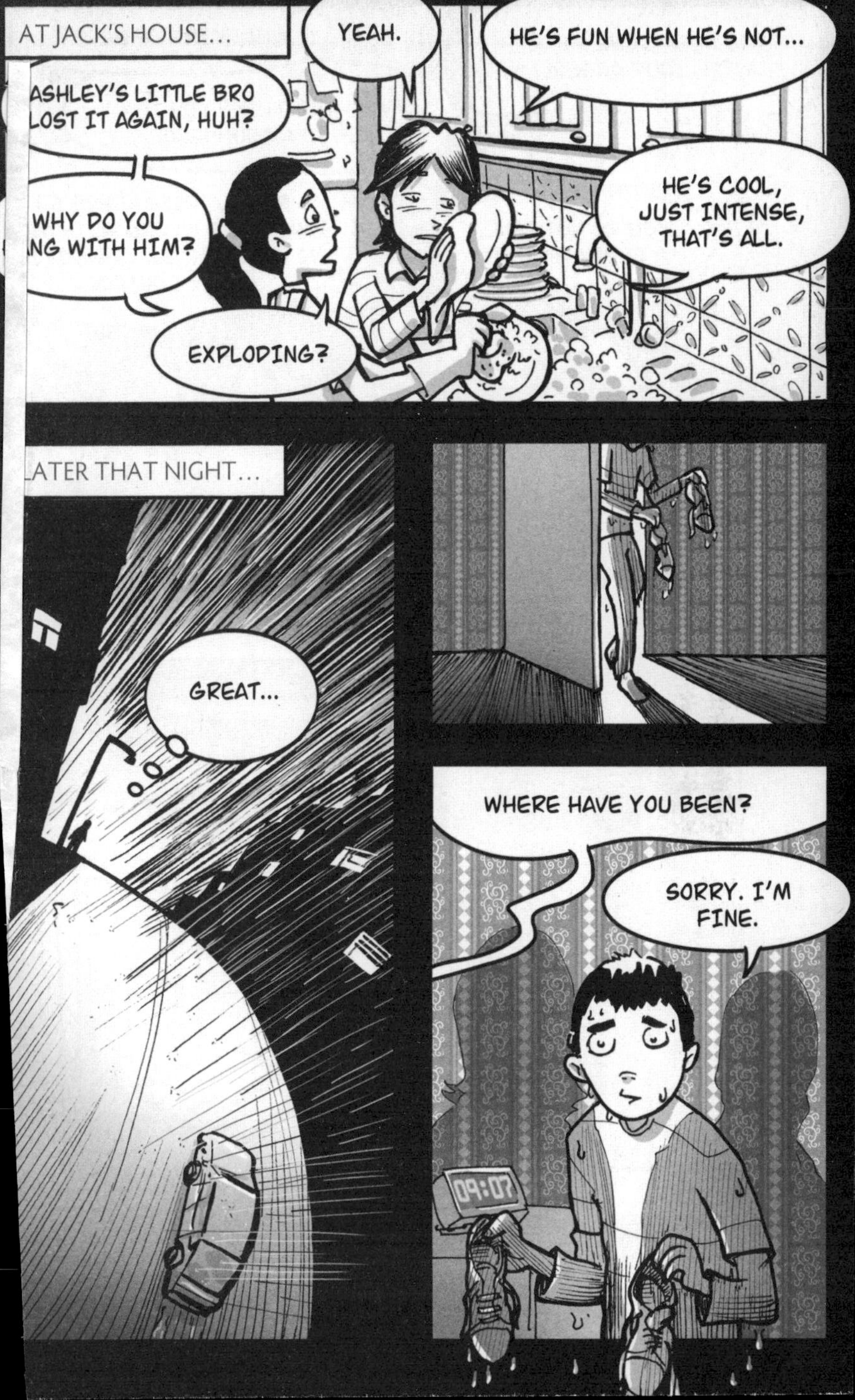
AT JACK'S HOUSE...
ASHLEY'S LITTLE BRO LOST IT AGAIN, HUH?
WHY DO YOU
NG WITH HIM?
YEAH.
HE'S FUN WHEN HE'S NOT...
EXPLODING?
HE'S COOL, JUST INTENSE, THAT'S ALL.
LATER THAT NIGHT...
GREAT...
WHERE HAVE YOU BEEN?
SORRY. I'M FINE.
09:07

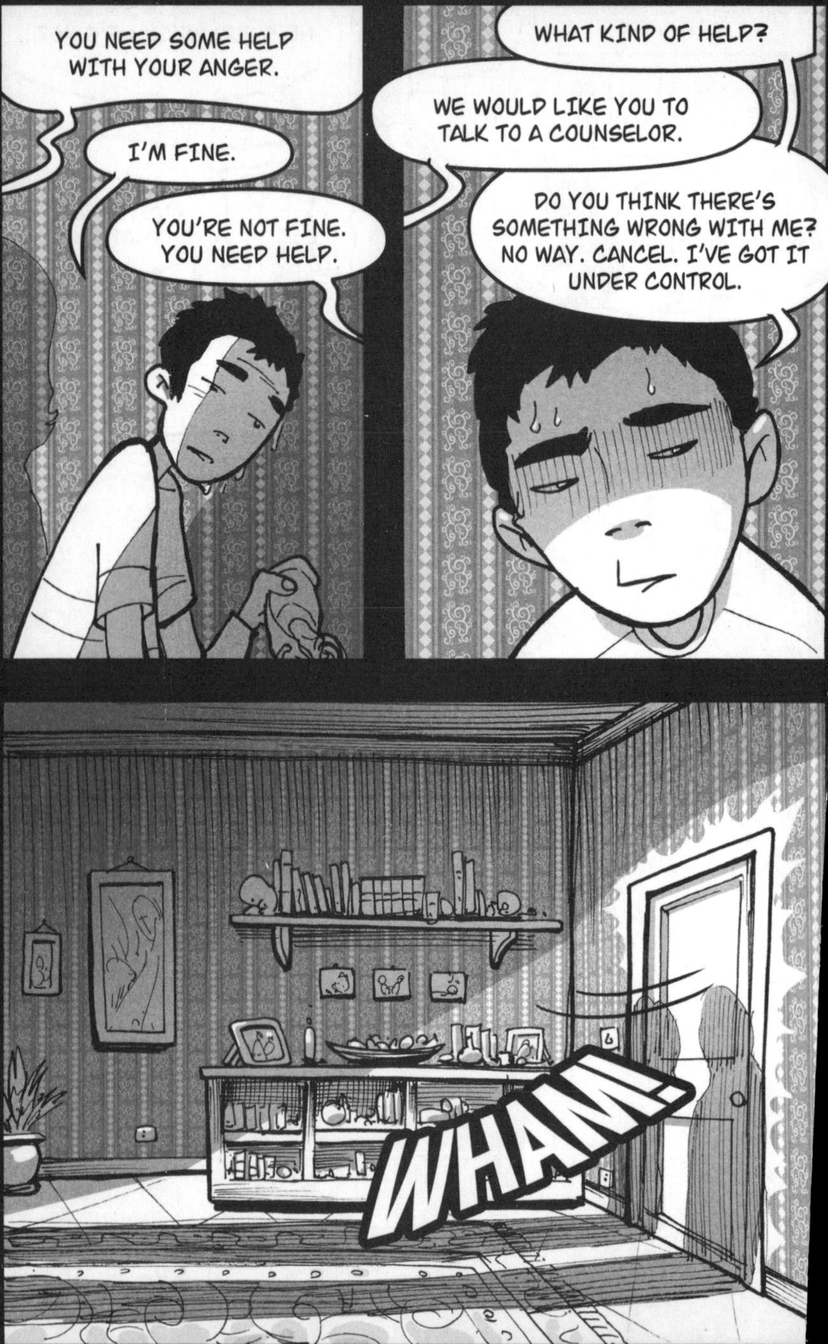
YOU NEED SOME HELP WITH YOUR ANGER.
I'M FINE.
YOU'RE NOT FINE. YOU NEED HELP.
WHAT KIND OF HELP?
WE WOULD LIKE YOU TO TALK TO A COUNSELOR.
DO YOU THINK THERE'S SOMETHING WRONG WITH ME? NO WAY. CANCEL. I'VE GOT IT UNDER CONTROL.
WHAM!

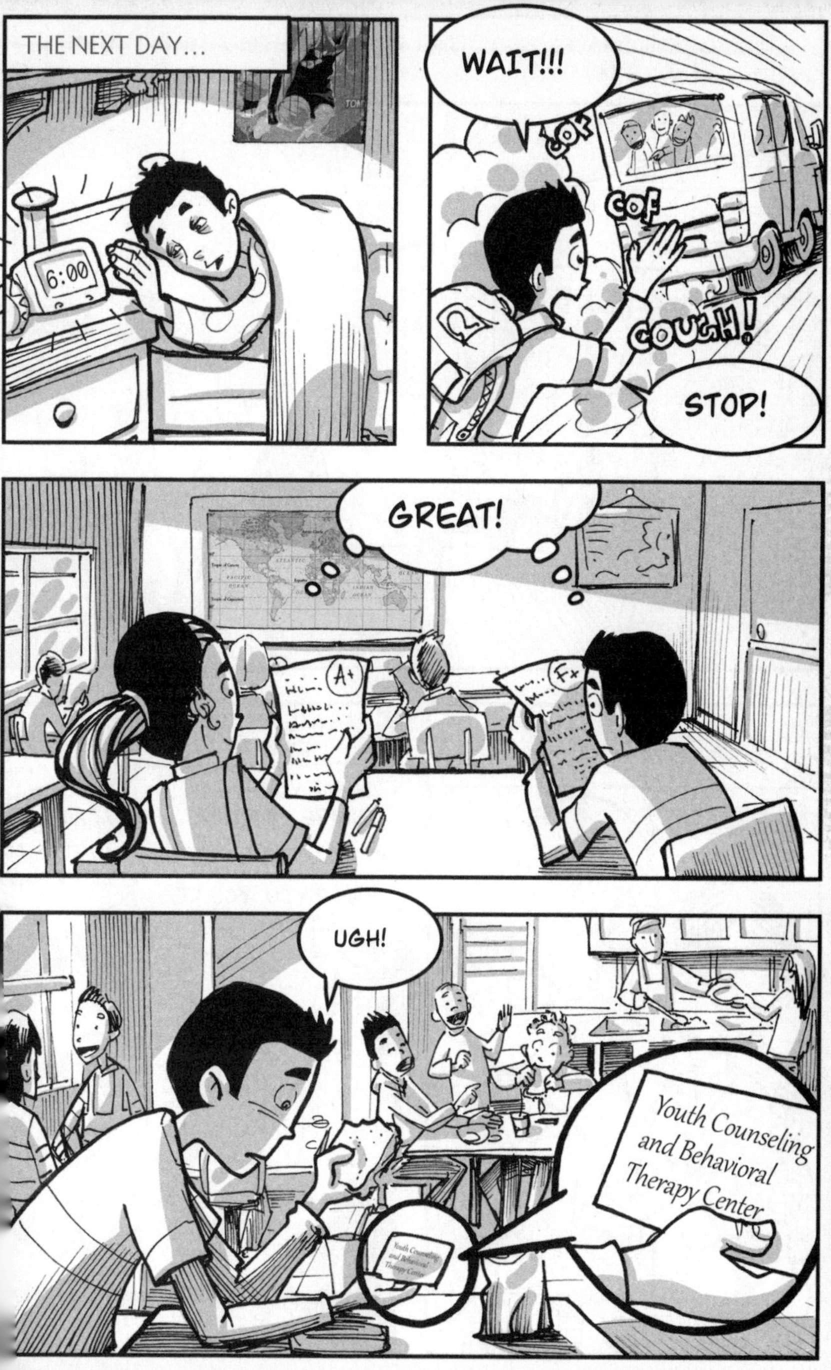
THE NEXT DAY…
6:00
WAIT!!!
COF
COF
COUGH!
STOP!
GREAT!
A+
F
UGH!
Youth Counseling and Behavioral Therapy Center
Youth Counseling and Behavioral Therapy Center

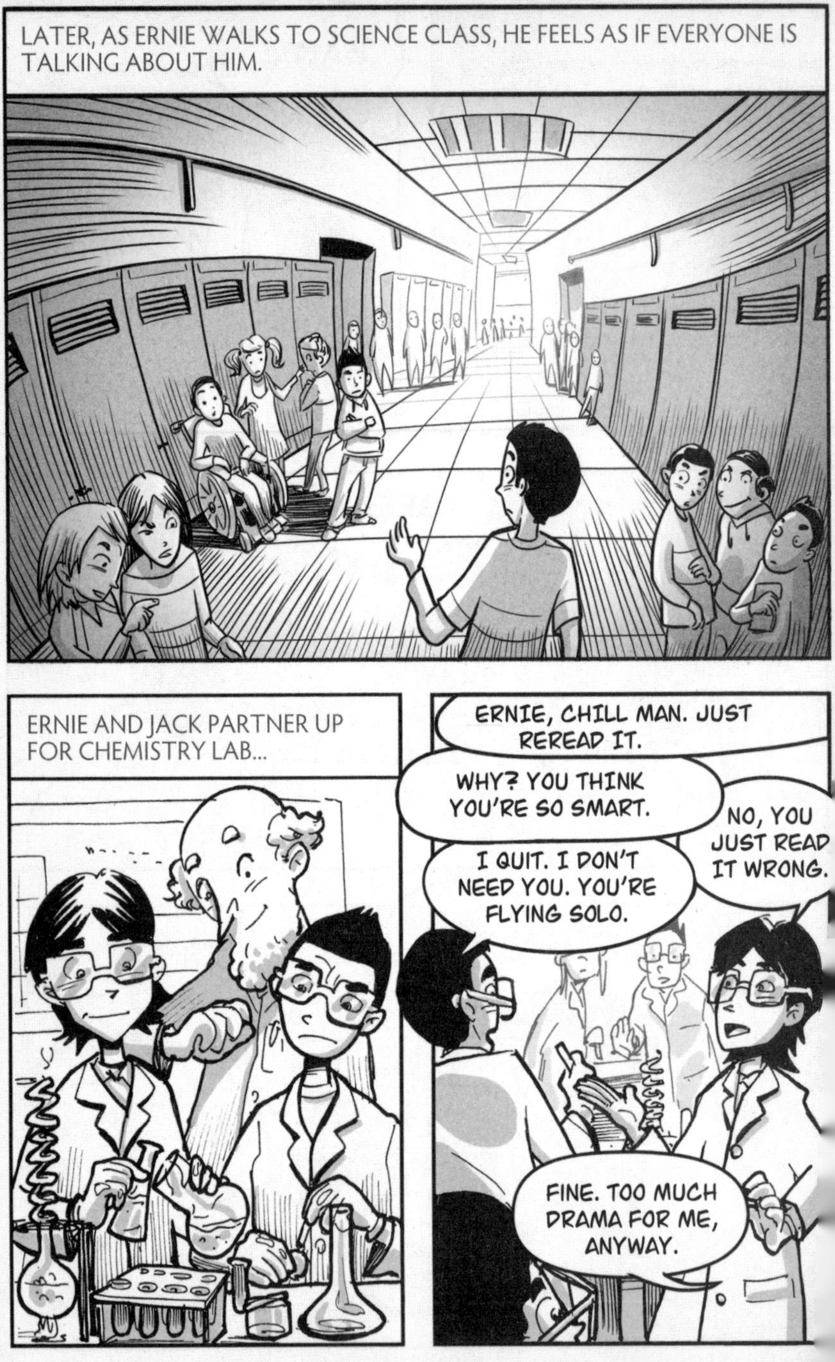
LATER, AS ERNIE WALKS TO SCIENCE CLASS, HE FEELS AS IF EVERYONE IS TALKING ABOUT HIM.
ERNIE AND JACK PARTNER UP FOR CHEMISTRY LAB...
ERNIE, CHILL MAN. JUST REREAD IT.
WHY? YOU THINK YOU'RE SO SMART.
NO, YOU JUST READ IT WRONG.
I QUIT. I DON'T NEED YOU. YOU'RE FLYING SOLO.
FINE. TOO MUCH DRAMA FOR ME, ANYWAY.

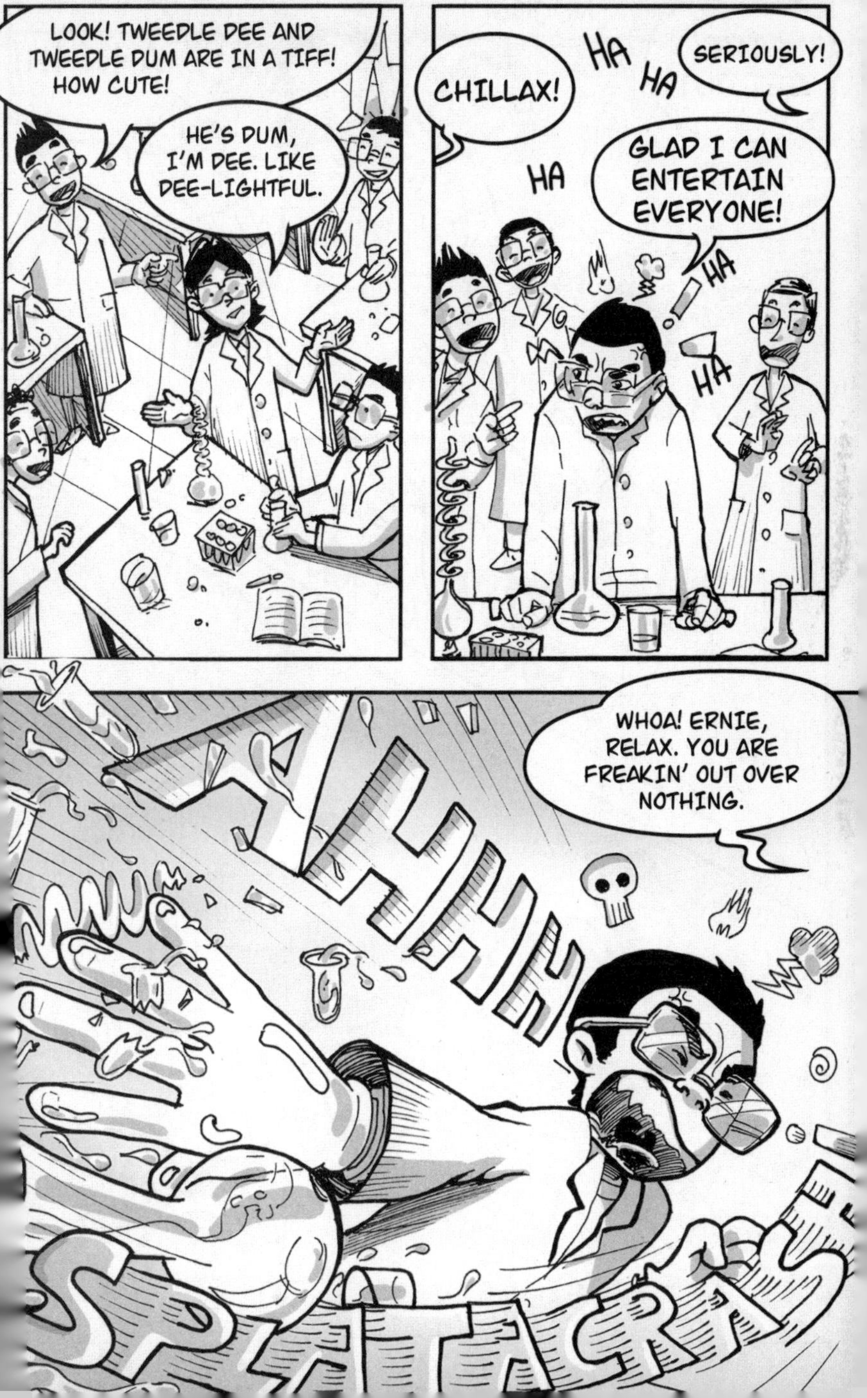
LOOK! TWEEDLE DEE AND TWEEDLE DUM ARE IN A TIFF! HOW CUTE!
HE'S DUM, I'M DEE. LIKE DEE-LIGHTFUL.
CHILLAX!
HA HA
SERIOUSLY!
HA
GLAD I CAN ENTERTAIN EVERYONE!
HA
HA
WHOA! ERNIE, RELAX. YOU ARE FREAKIN' OUT OVER NOTHING.

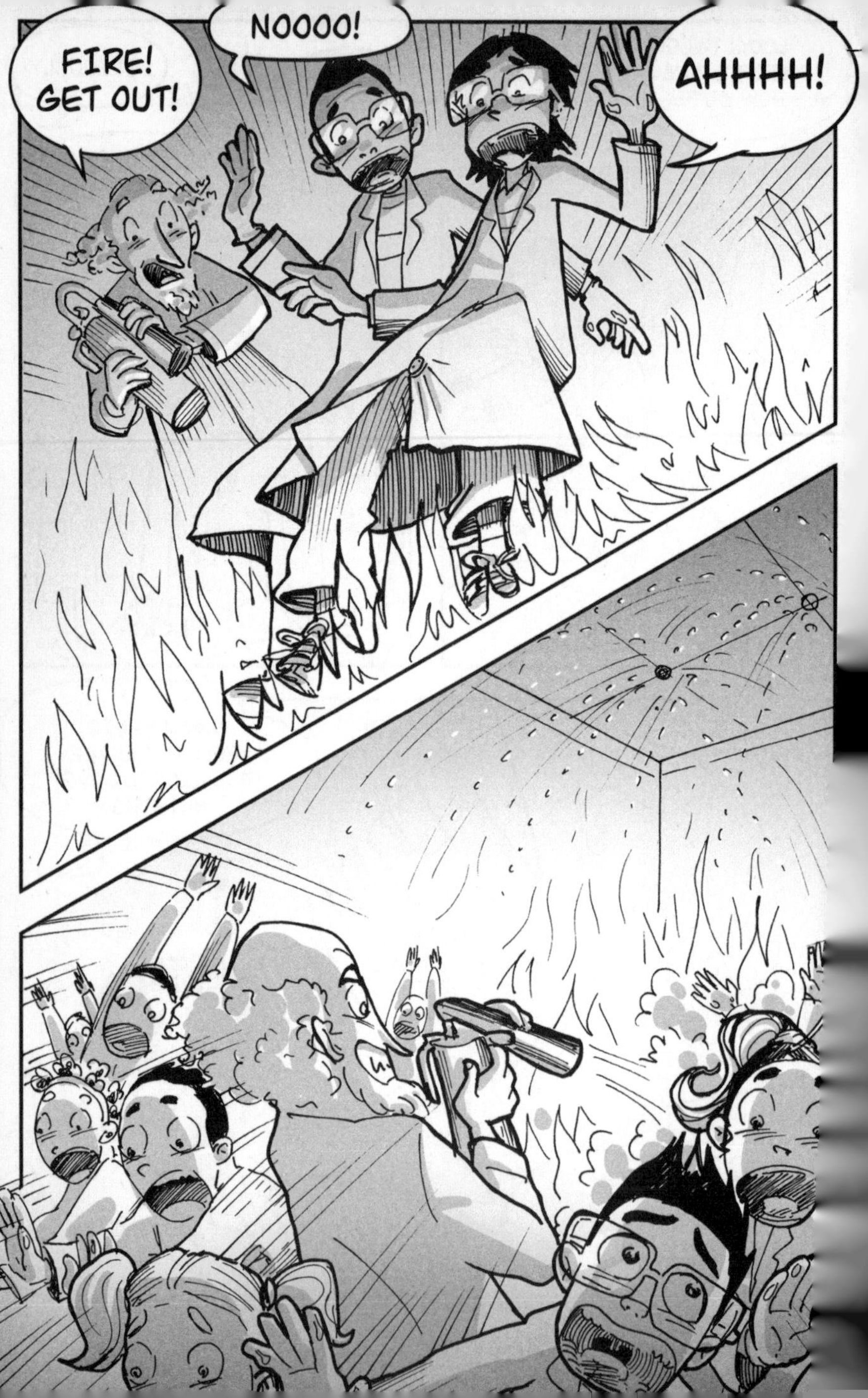
FIRE!
GET OUT!
NOOOO!
AHHHH!

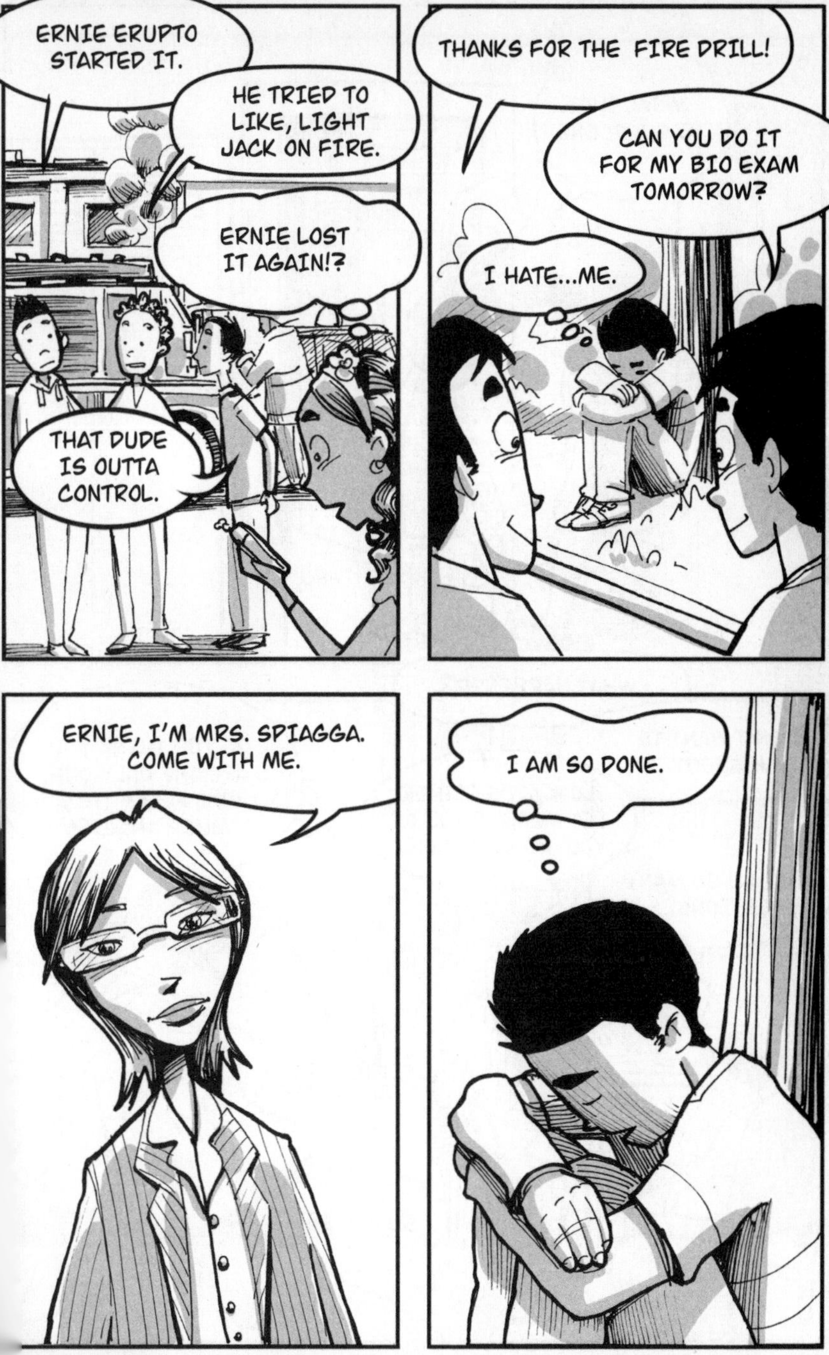
ERNIE ERUPTO STARTED IT.
HE TRIED TO LIKE, LIGHT JACK ON FIRE.
ERNIE LOST IT AGAIN!?
THAT DUDE IS OUTTA CONTROL.
THANKS FOR THE FIRE DRILL!
CAN YOU DO IT FOR MY BIO EXAM TOMORROW?
I HATE...ME.
ERNIE, I'M MRS. SPIAGGA. COME WITH ME.
I AM SO DONE.

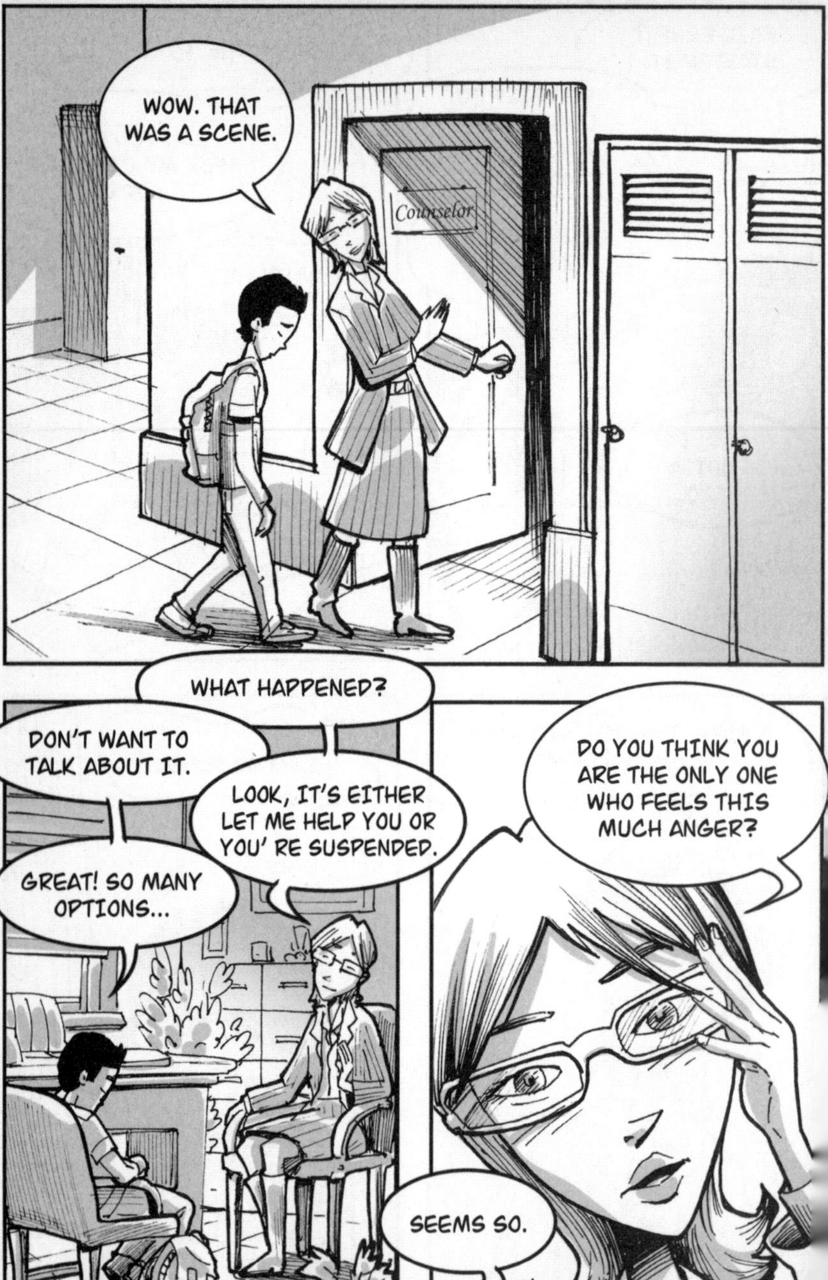
WOW. THAT WAS A SCENE.
Counselor
WHAT HAPPENED?
DON'T WANT TO TALK ABOUT IT.
LOOK, IT'S EITHER LET ME HELP YOU OR YOU' RE SUSPENDED.
GREAT! SO MANY OPTIONS...
DO YOU THINK YOU ARE THE ONLY ONE WHO FEELS THIS MUCH ANGER?
SEEMS SO.

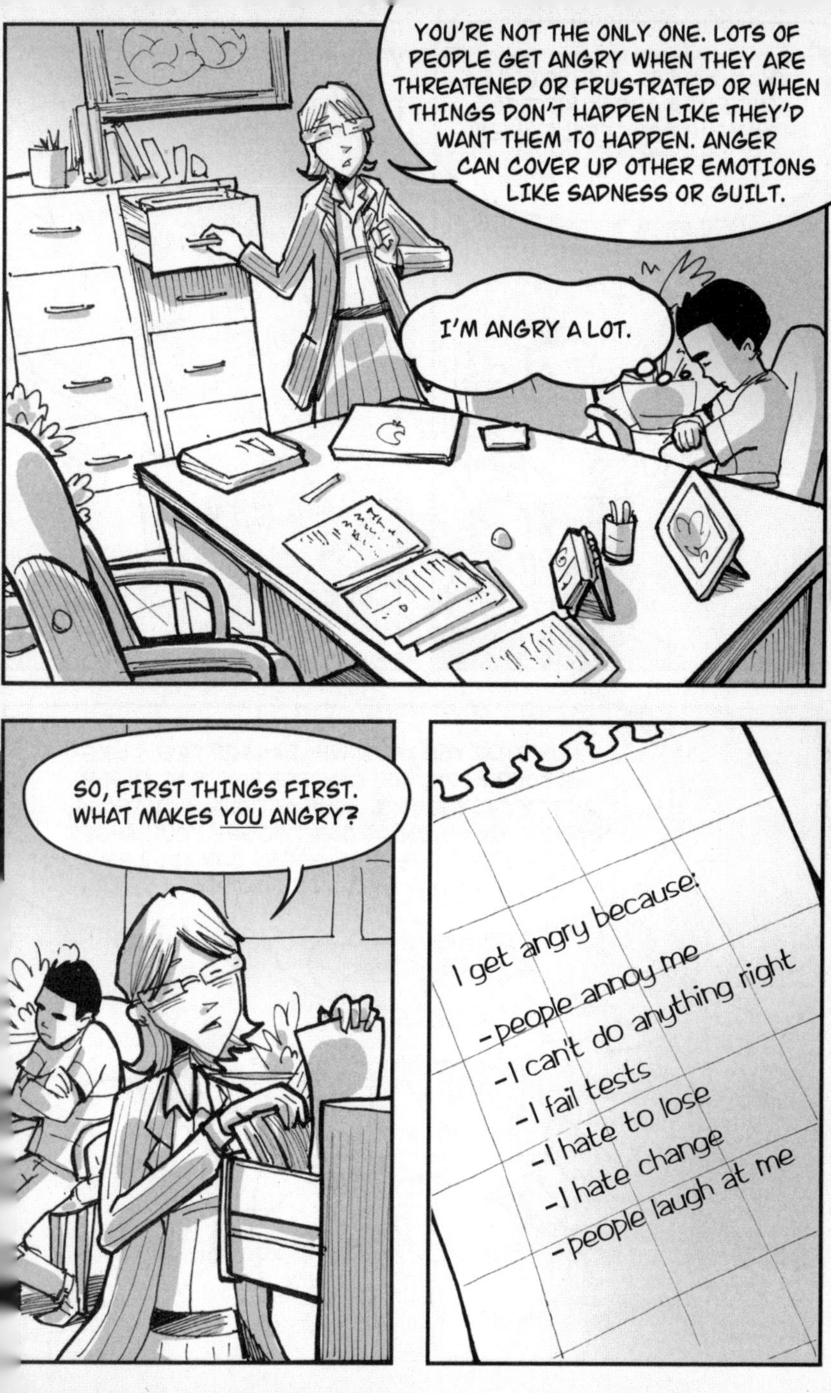
YOU'RE NOT THE ONLY ONE. LOTS OF PEOPLE GET ANGRY WHEN THEY ARE THREATENED OR FRUSTRATED OR WHEN THINGS DON'T HAPPEN LIKE THEY'D WANT THEM TO HAPPEN. ANGER CAN COVER UP OTHER EMOTIONS LIKE SADNESS OR GUILT.
I'M ANGRY A LOT.
SO, FIRST THINGS FIRST. WHAT MAKES YOU ANGRY?
I get angry because:
-people annoy me
-I can't do anything right
-I fail tests
-I hate to lose
-I hate change
-people laugh at me

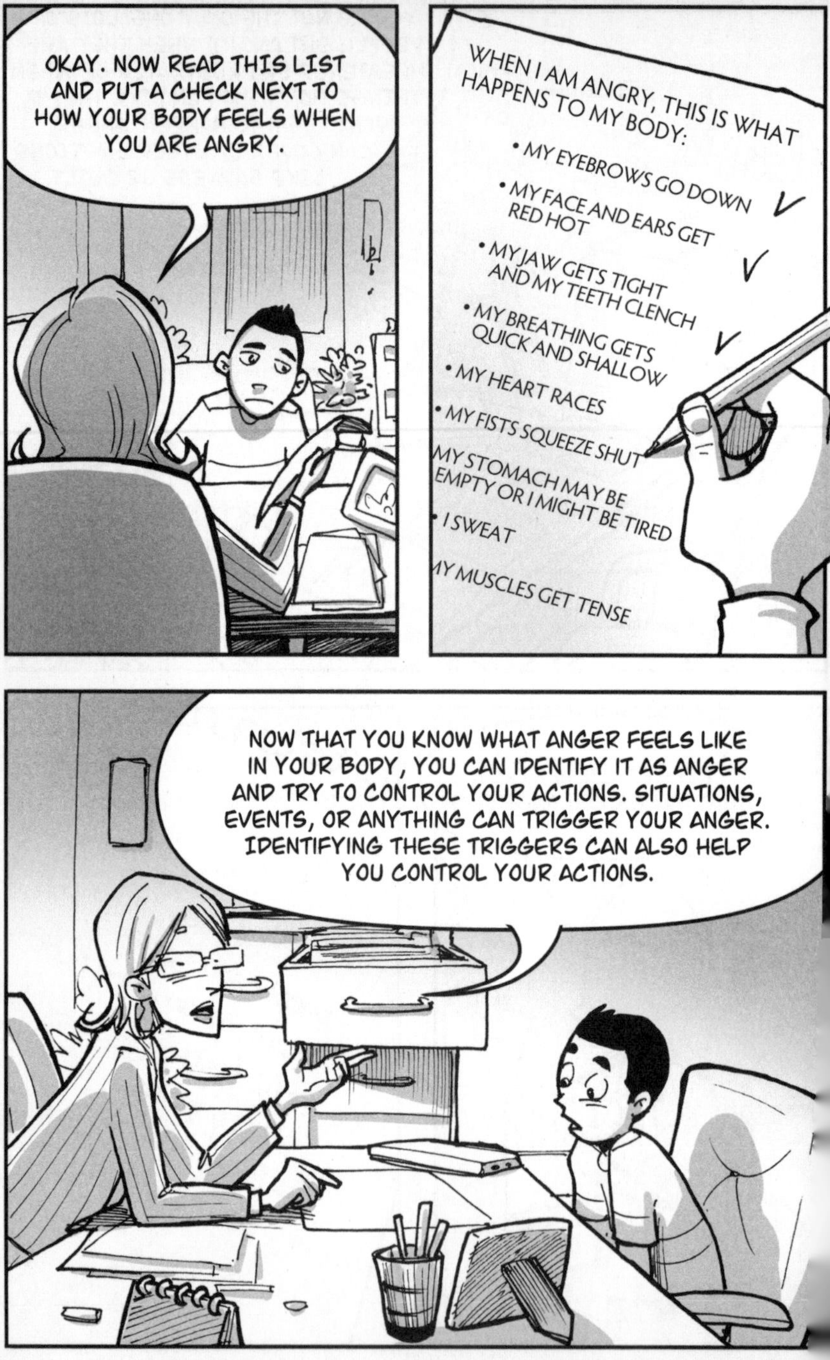

OKAY. NOW READ THIS LIST AND PUT A CHECK NEXT TO HOW YOUR BODY FEELS WHEN YOU ARE ANGRY.
WHEN I AM ANGRY, THIS IS WHAT HAPPENS TO MY BODY:
• MY EYEBROWS GO DOWN ✓
• MY FACE AND EARS GET RED HOT ✓
• MY JAW GETS TIGHT AND MY TEETH CLENCH ✓
• MY BREATHING GETS QUICK AND SHALLOW
• MY HEART RACES
• MY FISTS SQUEEZE SHUT
MY STOMACH MAY BE EMPTY OR I MIGHT BE TIRED
• I SWEAT
MY MUSCLES GET TENSE
NOW THAT YOU KNOW WHAT ANGER FEELS LIKE IN YOUR BODY, YOU CAN IDENTIFY IT AS ANGER AND TRY TO CONTROL YOUR ACTIONS. SITUATIONS, EVENTS, OR ANYTHING CAN TRIGGER YOUR ANGER. IDENTIFYING THESE TRIGGERS CAN ALSO HELP YOU CONTROL YOUR ACTIONS.

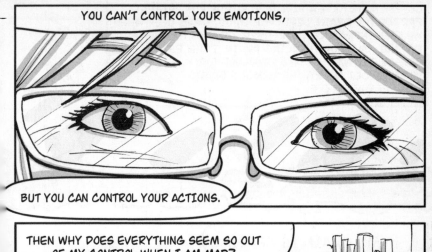

YOU CAN'T CONTROL YOUR EMOTIONS,

BUT YOU CAN CONTROL YOUR ACTIONS.

THEN WHY DOES EVERYTHING SEEM SO OUT OF MY CONTROL WHEN I AM MAD?

NEW BRAIN THINKS. OLD BRAIN SURVIVES.

THERE IS A PART OF OUR BRAINS LEFT OVER FROM THE TIME OF THE CAVEMEN. IT ONLY KNOWS HOW TO SURVIVE A THREAT, AND IT TAKES OVER WHEN WE ARE ANGRY. IT IS HARD TO THINK OUR WAY OUT OF A PROBLEM WHEN THE OLD BRAIN IS ON.

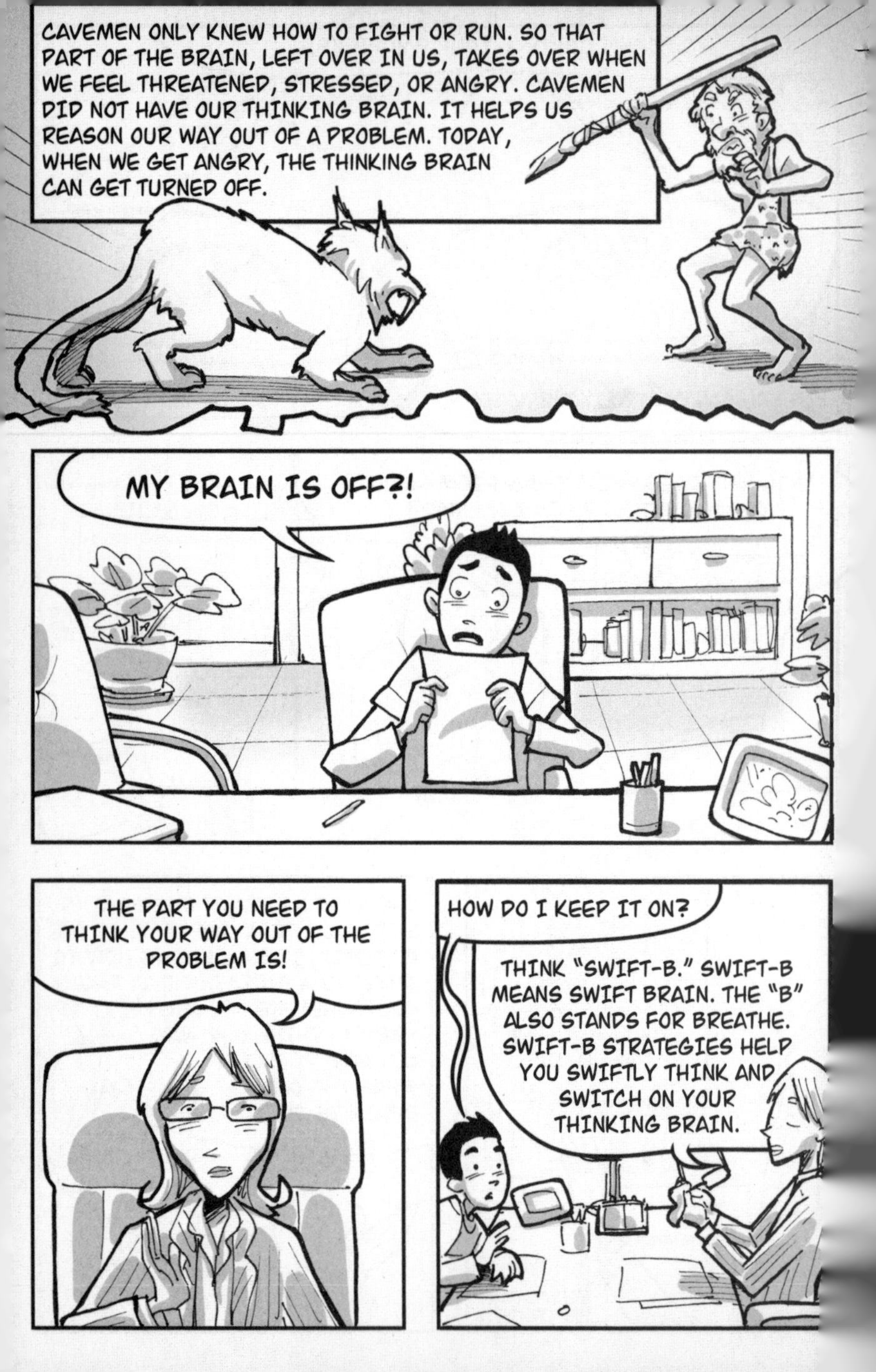
CAVEMEN ONLY KNEW HOW TO FIGHT OR RUN. SO THAT PART OF THE BRAIN, LEFT OVER IN US, TAKES OVER WHEN WE FEEL THREATENED, STRESSED, OR ANGRY. CAVEMEN DID NOT HAVE OUR THINKING BRAIN. IT HELPS US REASON OUR WAY OUT OF A PROBLEM. TODAY, WHEN WE GET ANGRY, THE THINKING BRAIN CAN GET TURNED OFF.
MY BRAIN IS OFF?!
THE PART YOU NEED TO THINK YOUR WAY OUT OF THE PROBLEM IS!
HOW DO I KEEP IT ON?
THINK "SWIFT-B." SWIFT-B MEANS SWIFT BRAIN. THE "B" ALSO STANDS FOR BREATHE. SWIFT-B STRATEGIES HELP YOU SWIFTLY THINK AND SWITCH ON YOUR THINKING BRAIN.

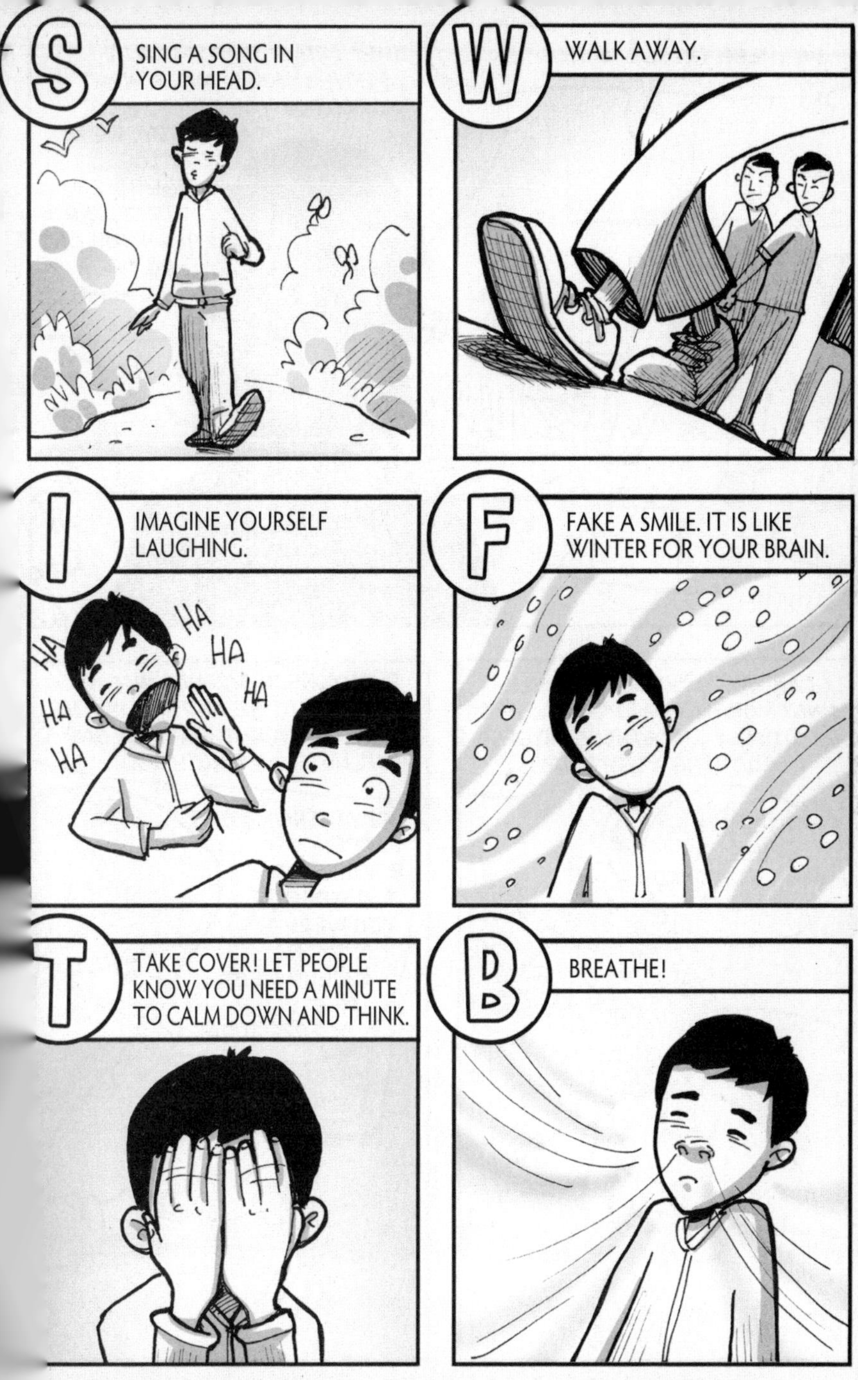
S
SING A SONG IN YOUR HEAD.
W
WALK AWAY.
I
IMAGINE YOURSELF LAUGHING.
HA HA HA HA HA HA
F
FAKE A SMILE. IT IS LIKE WINTER FOR YOUR BRAIN.
T
TAKE COVER! LET PEOPLE KNOW YOU NEED A MINUTE TO CALM DOWN AND THINK.
B
BREATHE!

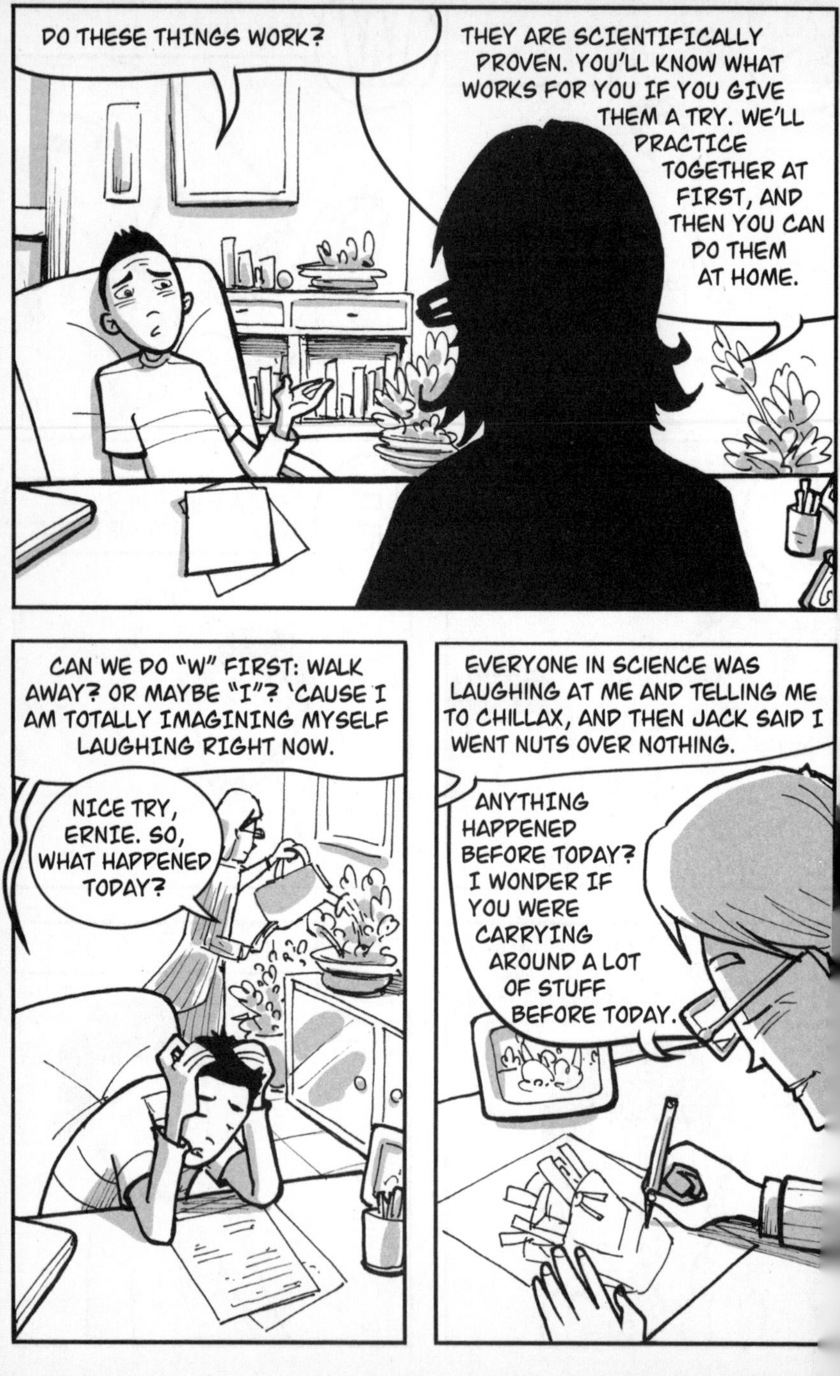
DO THESE THINGS WORK?
THEY ARE SCIENTIFICALLY PROVEN. YOU'LL KNOW WHAT WORKS FOR YOU IF YOU GIVE THEM A TRY. WE'LL PRACTICE TOGETHER AT FIRST, AND THEN YOU CAN DO THEM AT HOME.
CAN WE DO "W" FIRST: WALK AWAY? OR MAYBE "I"? 'CAUSE I AM TOTALLY IMAGINING MYSELF LAUGHING RIGHT NOW.
NICE TRY, ERNIE. SO, WHAT HAPPENED TODAY?
EVERYONE IN SCIENCE WAS LAUGHING AT ME AND TELLING ME TO CHILLAX, AND THEN JACK SAID I WENT NUTS OVER NOTHING.
ANYTHING HAPPENED BEFORE TODAY? I WONDER IF YOU WERE CARRYING AROUND A LOT OF STUFF BEFORE TODAY.

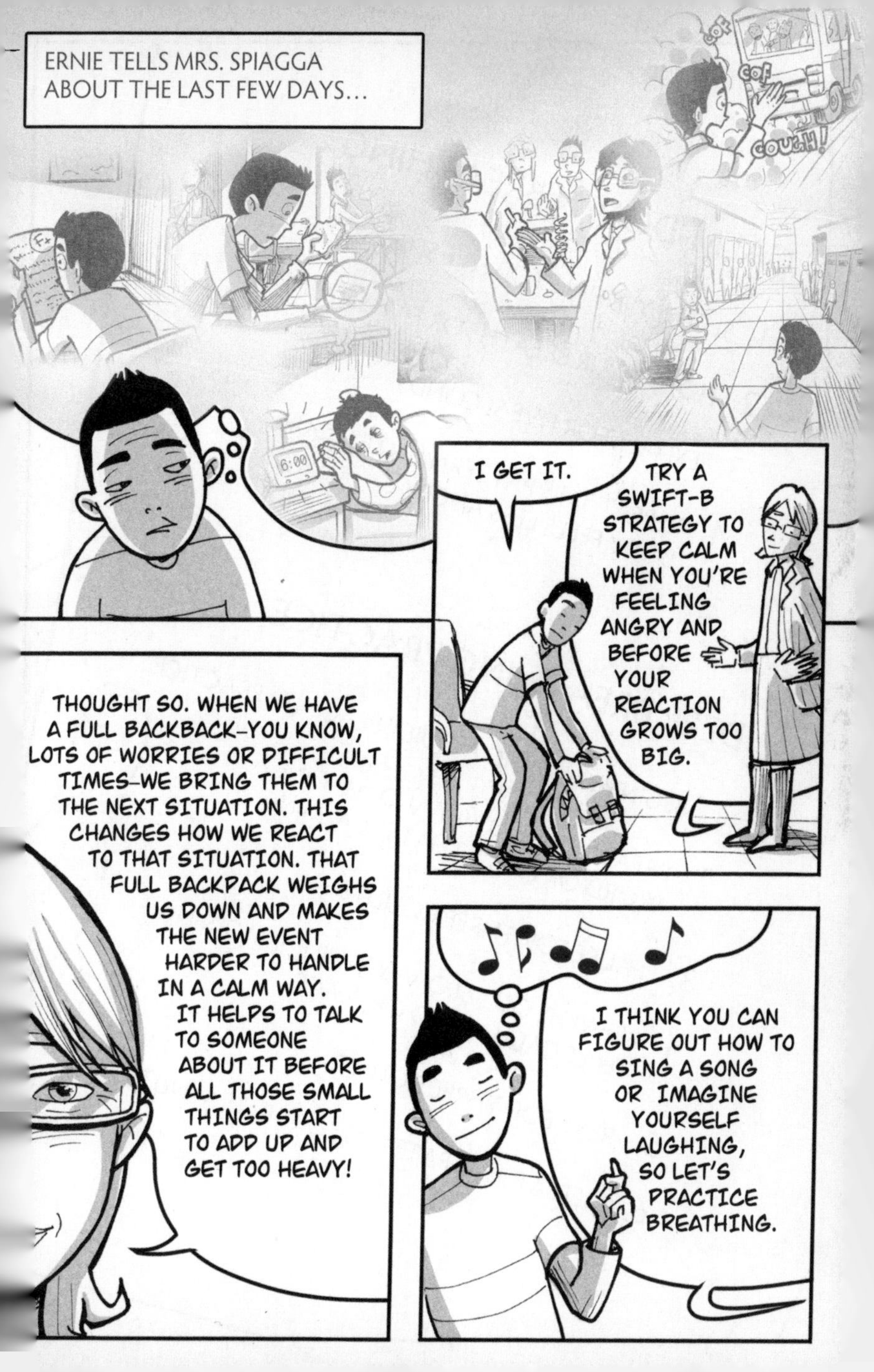

ERNIE TELLS MRS. SPIAGGA ABOUT THE LAST FEW DAYS...
COF
COF
COUGH!
6:00
I GET IT.
TRY A SWIFT-B STRATEGY TO KEEP CALM WHEN YOU'RE FEELING ANGRY AND BEFORE YOUR REACTION GROWS TOO BIG.
THOUGHT SO. WHEN WE HAVE A FULL BACKBACK–YOU KNOW, LOTS OF WORRIES OR DIFFICULT TIMES–WE BRING THEM TO THE NEXT SITUATION. THIS CHANGES HOW WE REACT TO THAT SITUATION. THAT FULL BACKPACK WEIGHS US DOWN AND MAKES THE NEW EVENT HARDER TO HANDLE IN A CALM WAY. IT HELPS TO TALK TO SOMEONE ABOUT IT BEFORE ALL THOSE SMALL THINGS START TO ADD UP AND GET TOO HEAVY!
I THINK YOU CAN FIGURE OUT HOW TO SING A SONG OR IMAGINE YOURSELF LAUGHING, SO LET'S PRACTICE BREATHING.

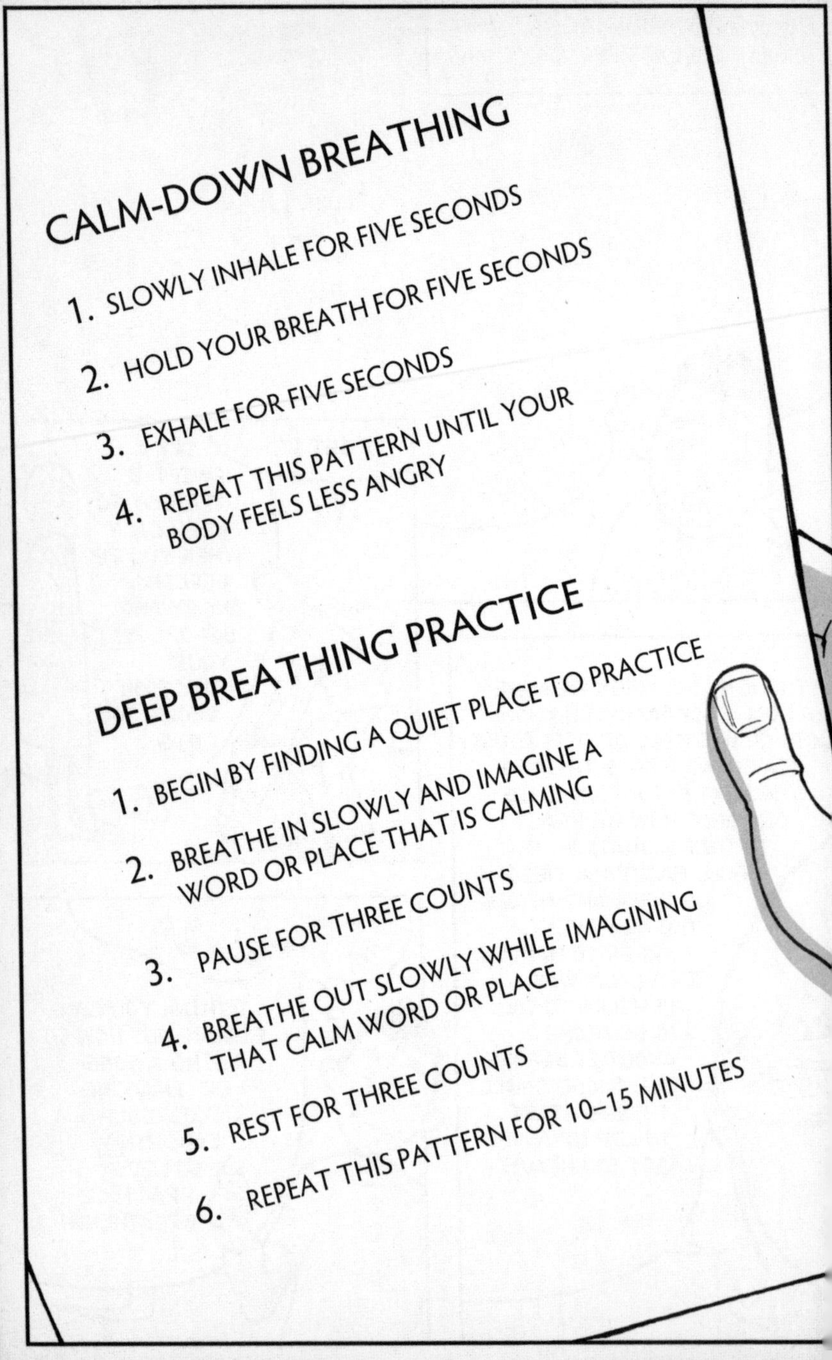
CALM-DOWN BREATHING
1. SLOWLY INHALE FOR FIVE SECONDS
2. HOLD YOUR BREATH FOR FIVE SECONDS
3. EXHALE FOR FIVE SECONDS
4. REPEAT THIS PATTERN UNTIL YOUR BODY FEELS LESS ANGRY
DEEP BREATHING PRACTICE
1. BEGIN BY FINDING A QUIET PLACE TO PRACTICE
2. BREATHE IN SLOWLY AND IMAGINE A WORD OR PLACE THAT IS CALMING
3. PAUSE FOR THREE COUNTS
4. BREATHE OUT SLOWLY WHILE IMAGINING THAT CALM WORD OR PLACE
5. REST FOR THREE COUNTS
6. REPEAT THIS PATTERN FOR 10–15 MINUTES

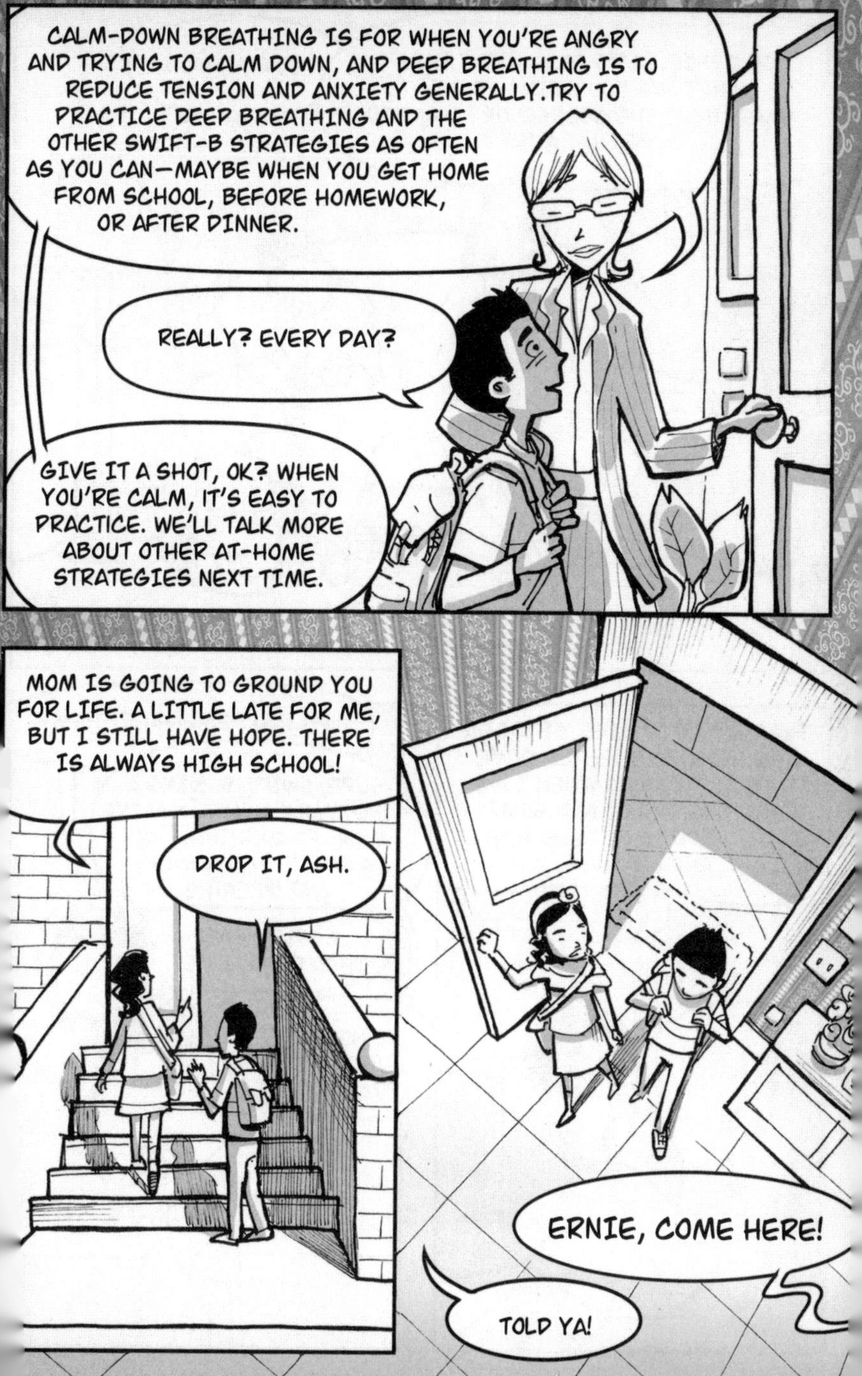
CALM-DOWN BREATHING IS FOR WHEN YOU'RE ANGRY AND TRYING TO CALM DOWN, AND DEEP BREATHING IS TO REDUCE TENSION AND ANXIETY GENERALLY. TRY TO PRACTICE DEEP BREATHING AND THE OTHER SWIFT-B STRATEGIES AS OFTEN AS YOU CAN—MAYBE WHEN YOU GET HOME FROM SCHOOL, BEFORE HOMEWORK, OR AFTER DINNER.
REALLY? EVERY DAY?
GIVE IT A SHOT, OK? WHEN YOU'RE CALM, IT'S EASY TO PRACTICE. WE'LL TALK MORE ABOUT OTHER AT-HOME STRATEGIES NEXT TIME.
MOM IS GOING TO GROUND YOU FOR LIFE. A LITTLE LATE FOR ME, BUT I STILL HAVE HOPE. THERE IS ALWAYS HIGH SCHOOL!
DROP IT, ASH.
ERNIE, COME HERE!
TOLD YA!

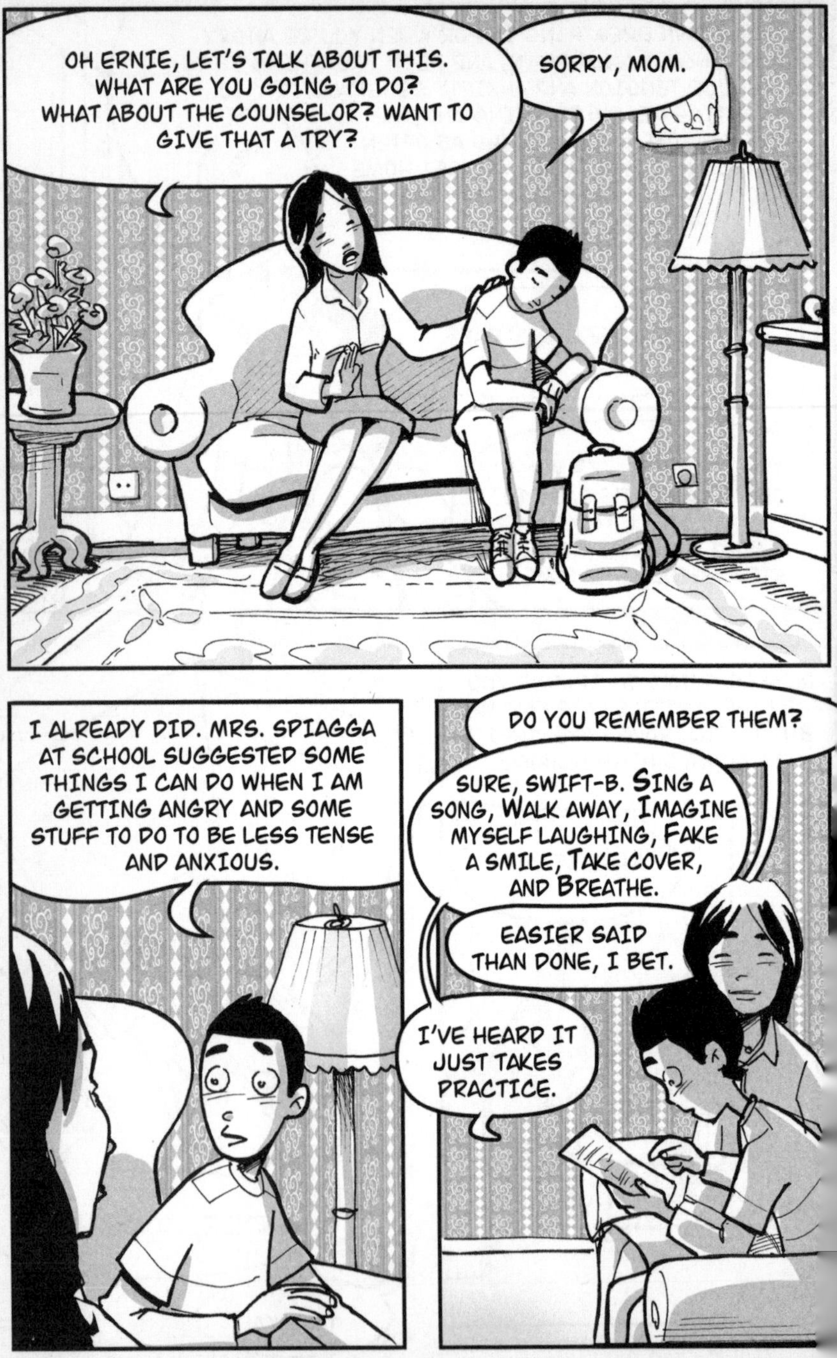
OH ERNIE, LET'S TALK ABOUT THIS. WHAT ARE YOU GOING TO DO? WHAT ABOUT THE COUNSELOR? WANT TO GIVE THAT A TRY?
SORRY, MOM.
I ALREADY DID. MRS. SPIAGGA AT SCHOOL SUGGESTED SOME THINGS I CAN DO WHEN I AM GETTING ANGRY AND SOME STUFF TO DO TO BE LESS TENSE AND ANXIOUS.
DO YOU REMEMBER THEM?
SURE, SWIFT-B. SING A SONG, WALK AWAY, IMAGINE MYSELF LAUGHING, FAKE A SMILE, TAKE COVER, AND BREATHE.
EASIER SAID THAN DONE, I BET.
I'VE HEARD IT JUST TAKES PRACTICE.

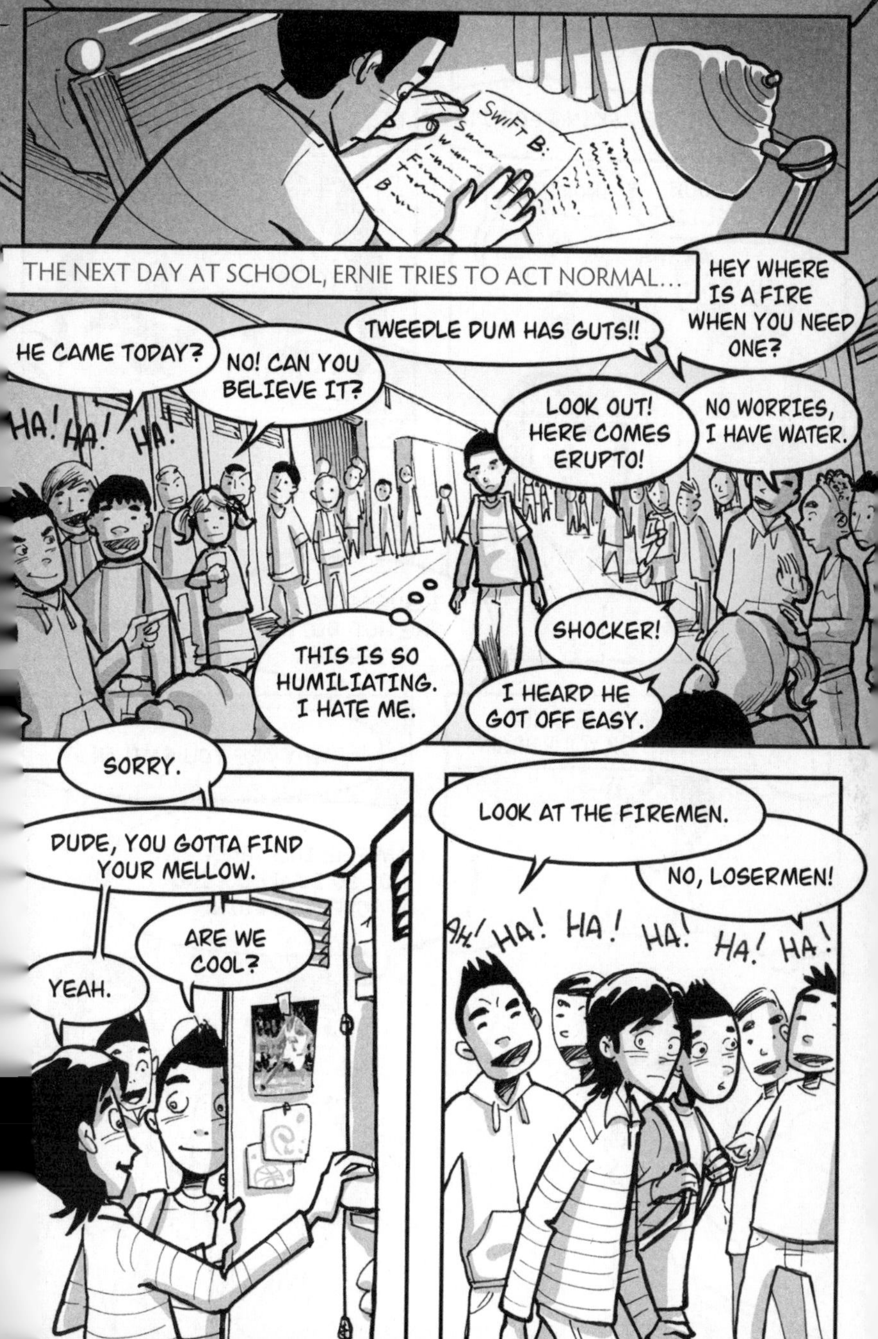
SWIFT B:
THE NEXT DAY AT SCHOOL, ERNIE TRIES TO ACT NORMAL…
HE CAME TODAY?
NO! CAN YOU BELIEVE IT?
HA! HA! HA!
TWEEDLE DUM HAS GUTS!!
HEY WHERE IS A FIRE WHEN YOU NEED ONE?
LOOK OUT! HERE COMES ERUPTO!
NO WORRIES, I HAVE WATER.
THIS IS SO HUMILIATING. I HATE ME.
SHOCKER!
I HEARD HE GOT OFF EASY.
SORRY.
DUDE, YOU GOTTA FIND YOUR MELLOW.
ARE WE COOL?
YEAH.
LOOK AT THE FIREMEN.
NO, LOSERMEN!
HA! HA! HA! HA! HA!

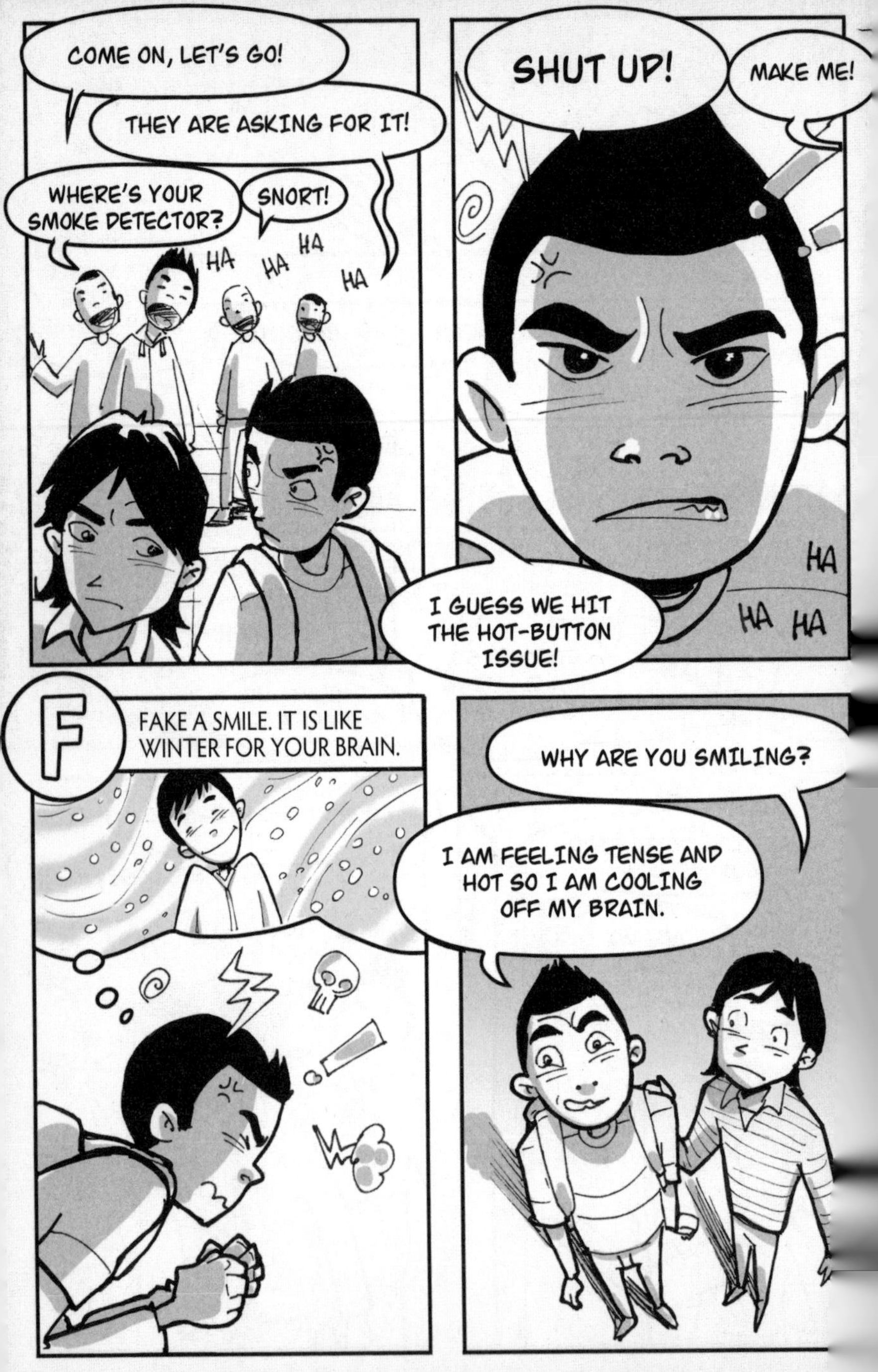
COME ON, LET'S GO!
THEY ARE ASKING FOR IT!
WHERE'S YOUR SMOKE DETECTOR?
SNORT!
HA HA HA HA
SHUT UP!
MAKE ME!
I GUESS WE HIT THE HOT-BUTTON ISSUE!
HA HA HA
F
FAKE A SMILE. IT IS LIKE WINTER FOR YOUR BRAIN.
WHY ARE YOU SMILING?
I AM FEELING TENSE AND HOT SO I AM COOLING OFF MY BRAIN.

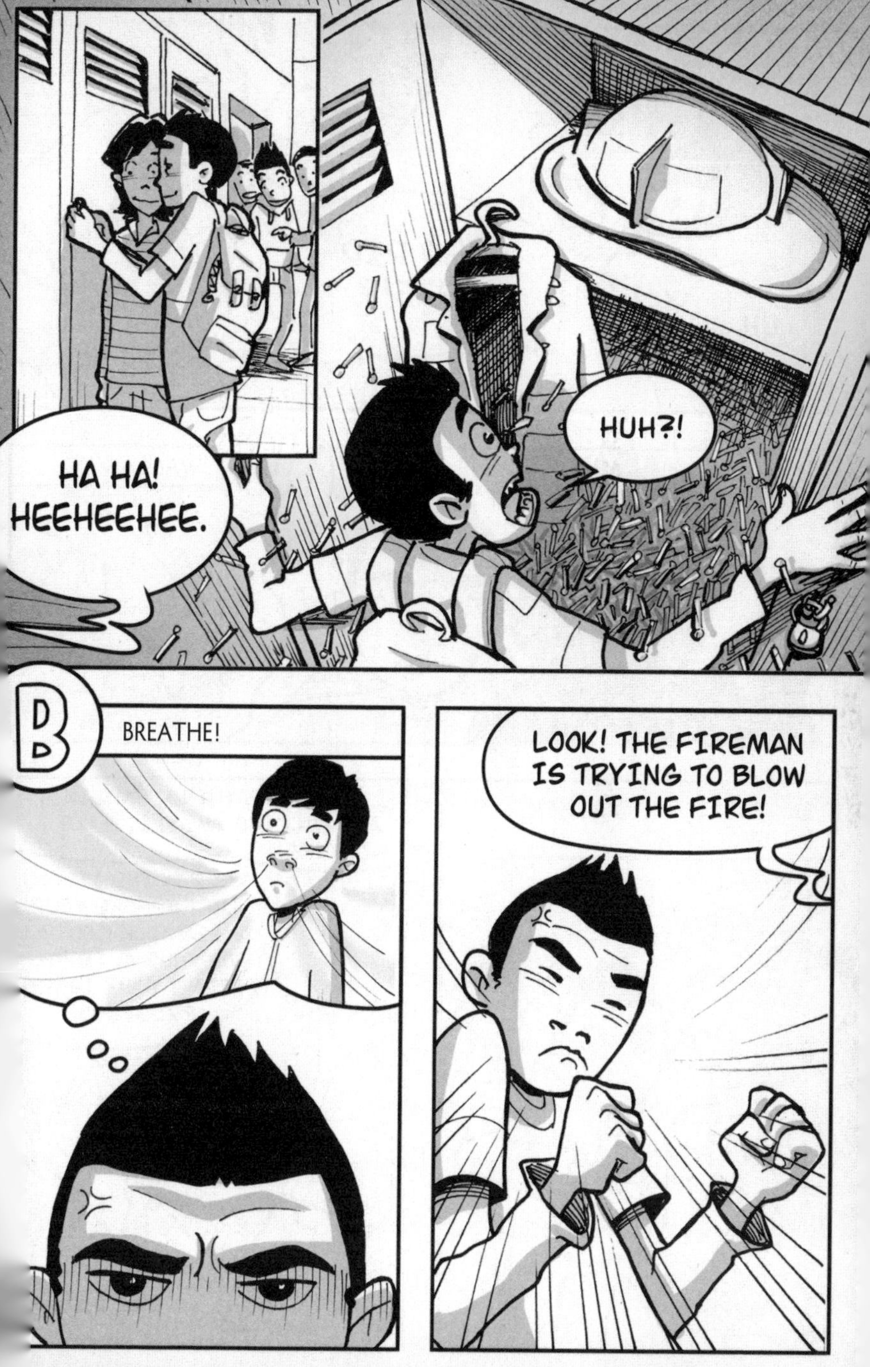
HA HA! HEEHEEHEE.
HUH?!
B
BREATHE!
LOOK! THE FIREMAN IS TRYING TO BLOW OUT THE FIRE!

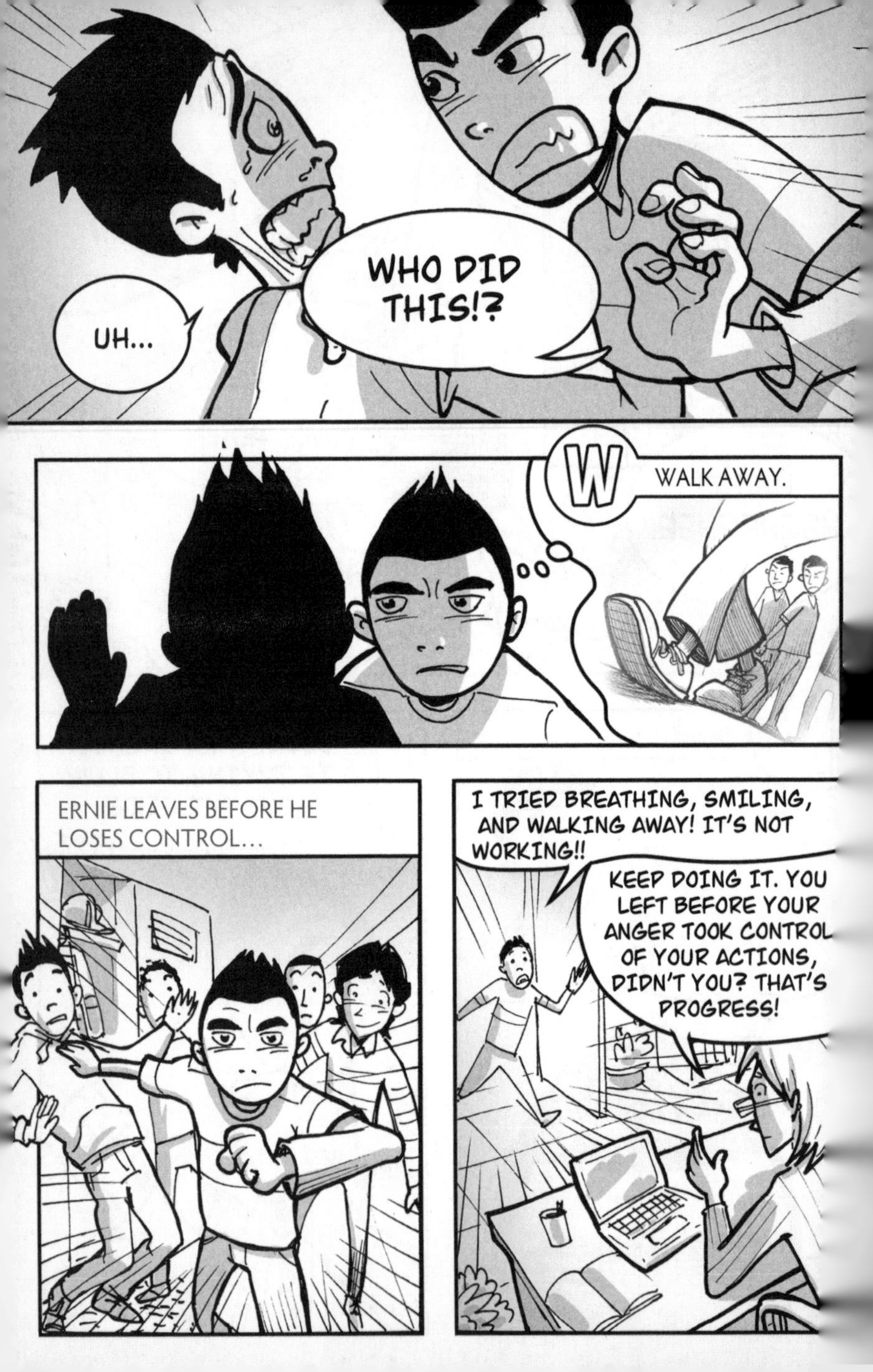
WHO DID THIS!?
UH...
WALK AWAY.
ERNIE LEAVES BEFORE HE LOSES CONTROL...
I TRIED BREATHING, SMILING, AND WALKING AWAY! IT'S NOT WORKING!!
KEEP DOING IT. YOU LEFT BEFORE YOUR ANGER TOOK CONTROL OF YOUR ACTIONS, DIDN'T YOU? THAT'S PROGRESS!

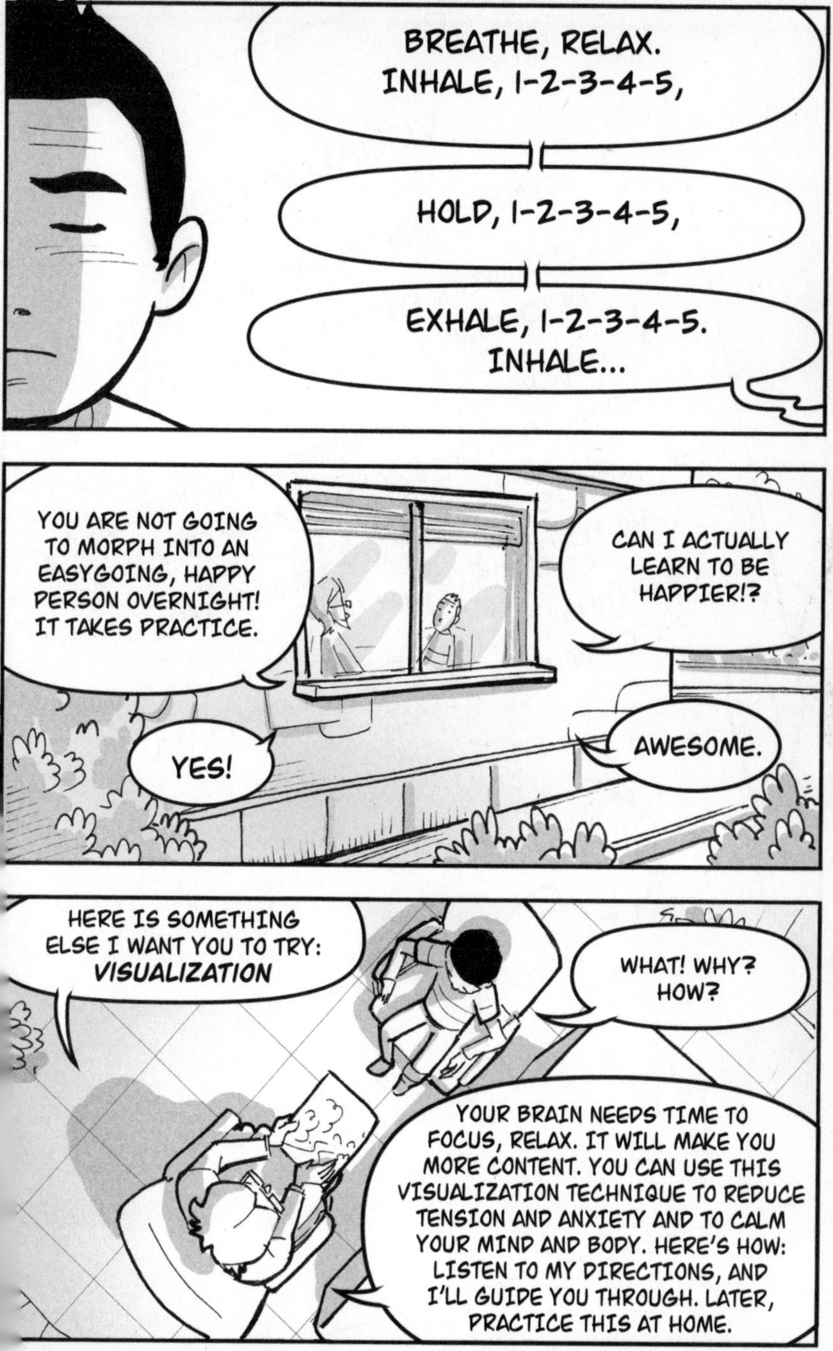
BREATHE, RELAX. INHALE, 1-2-3-4-5,
HOLD, 1-2-3-4-5,
EXHALE, 1-2-3-4-5. INHALE...
CAN I ACTUALLY LEARN TO BE HAPPIER!?
YOU ARE NOT GOING TO MORPH INTO AN EASYGOING, HAPPY PERSON OVERNIGHT! IT TAKES PRACTICE.
AWESOME.
YES!
HERE IS SOMETHING ELSE I WANT YOU TO TRY: VISUALIZATION
WHAT! WHY? HOW?
YOUR BRAIN NEEDS TIME TO FOCUS, RELAX. IT WILL MAKE YOU MORE CONTENT. YOU CAN USE THIS VISUALIZATION TECHNIQUE TO REDUCE TENSION AND ANXIETY AND TO CALM YOUR MIND AND BODY. HERE'S HOW: LISTEN TO MY DIRECTIONS, AND I'LL GUIDE YOU THROUGH. LATER, PRACTICE THIS AT HOME.

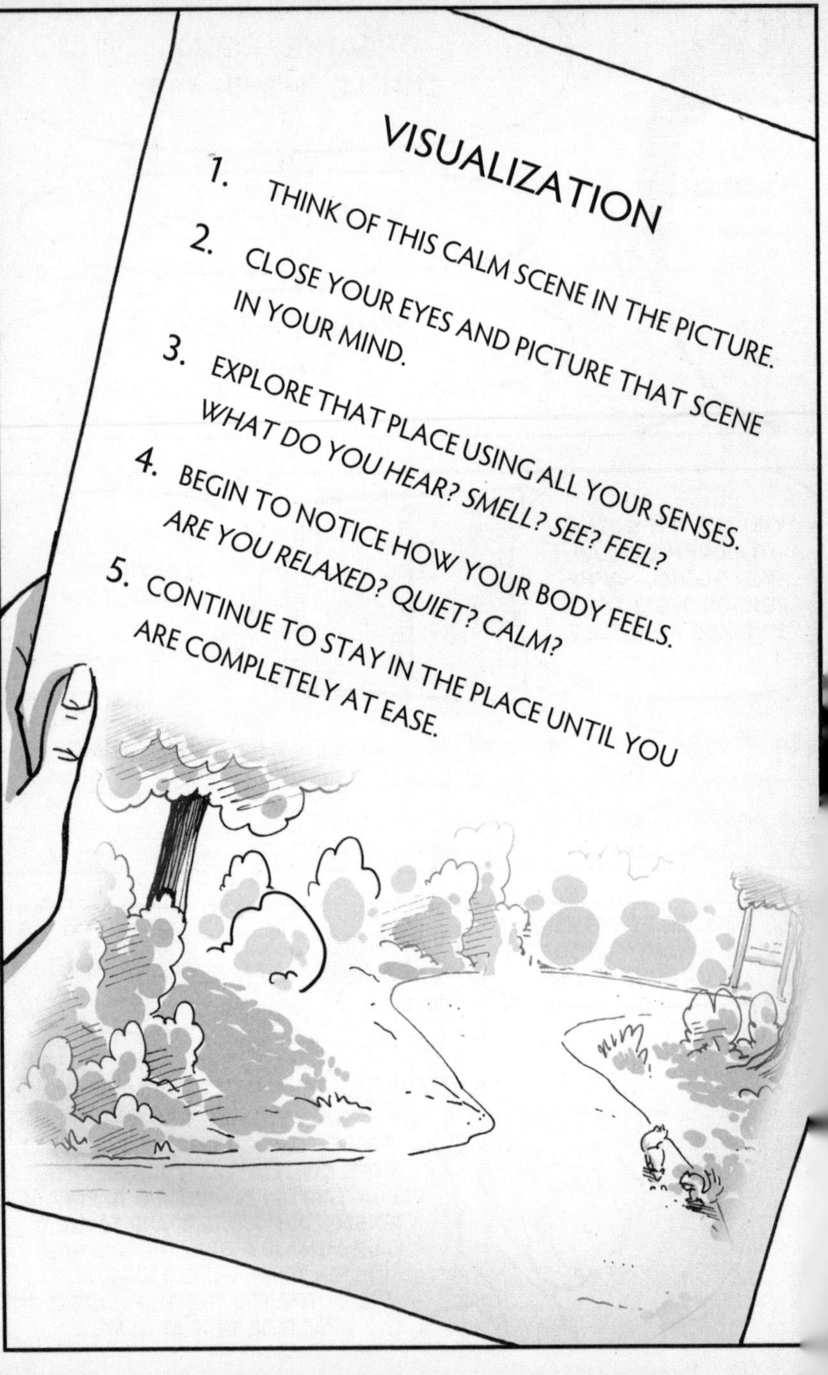
VISUALIZATION
1. THINK OF THIS CALM SCENE IN THE PICTURE.
2. CLOSE YOUR EYES AND PICTURE THAT SCENE IN YOUR MIND.
3. EXPLORE THAT PLACE USING ALL YOUR SENSES. WHAT DO YOU HEAR? SMELL? SEE? FEEL?
4. BEGIN TO NOTICE HOW YOUR BODY FEELS. ARE YOU RELAXED? QUIET? CALM?
5. CONTINUE TO STAY IN THE PLACE UNTIL YOU ARE COMPLETELY AT EASE.

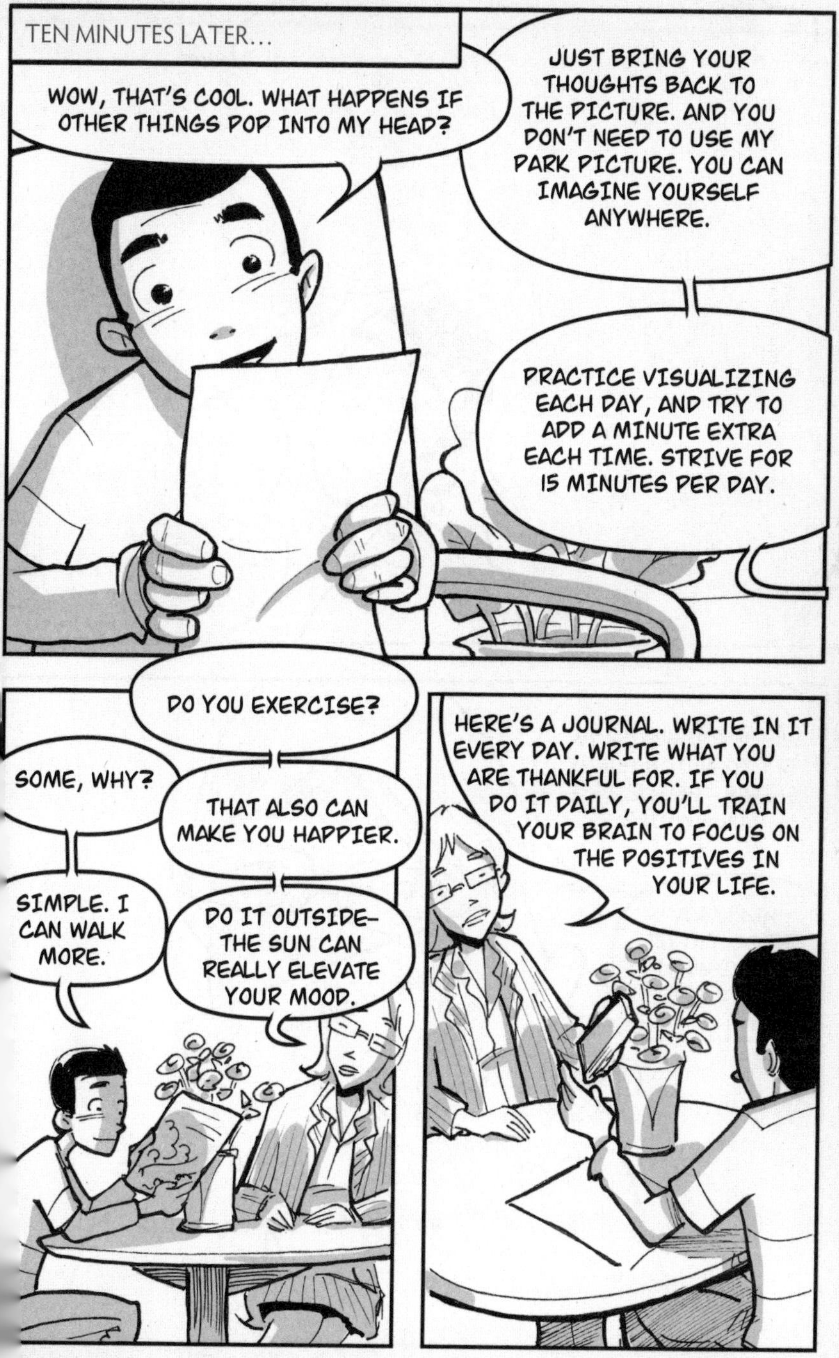
TEN MINUTES LATER...
WOW, THAT'S COOL. WHAT HAPPENS IF OTHER THINGS POP INTO MY HEAD?
JUST BRING YOUR THOUGHTS BACK TO THE PICTURE. AND YOU DON'T NEED TO USE MY PARK PICTURE. YOU CAN IMAGINE YOURSELF ANYWHERE.
PRACTICE VISUALIZING EACH DAY, AND TRY TO ADD A MINUTE EXTRA EACH TIME. STRIVE FOR 15 MINUTES PER DAY.
DO YOU EXERCISE?
SOME, WHY?
THAT ALSO CAN MAKE YOU HAPPIER.
SIMPLE. I CAN WALK MORE.
DO IT OUTSIDE—THE SUN CAN REALLY ELEVATE YOUR MOOD.
HERE'S A JOURNAL. WRITE IN IT EVERY DAY. WRITE WHAT YOU ARE THANKFUL FOR. IF YOU DO IT DAILY, YOU'LL TRAIN YOUR BRAIN TO FOCUS ON THE POSITIVES IN YOUR LIFE.

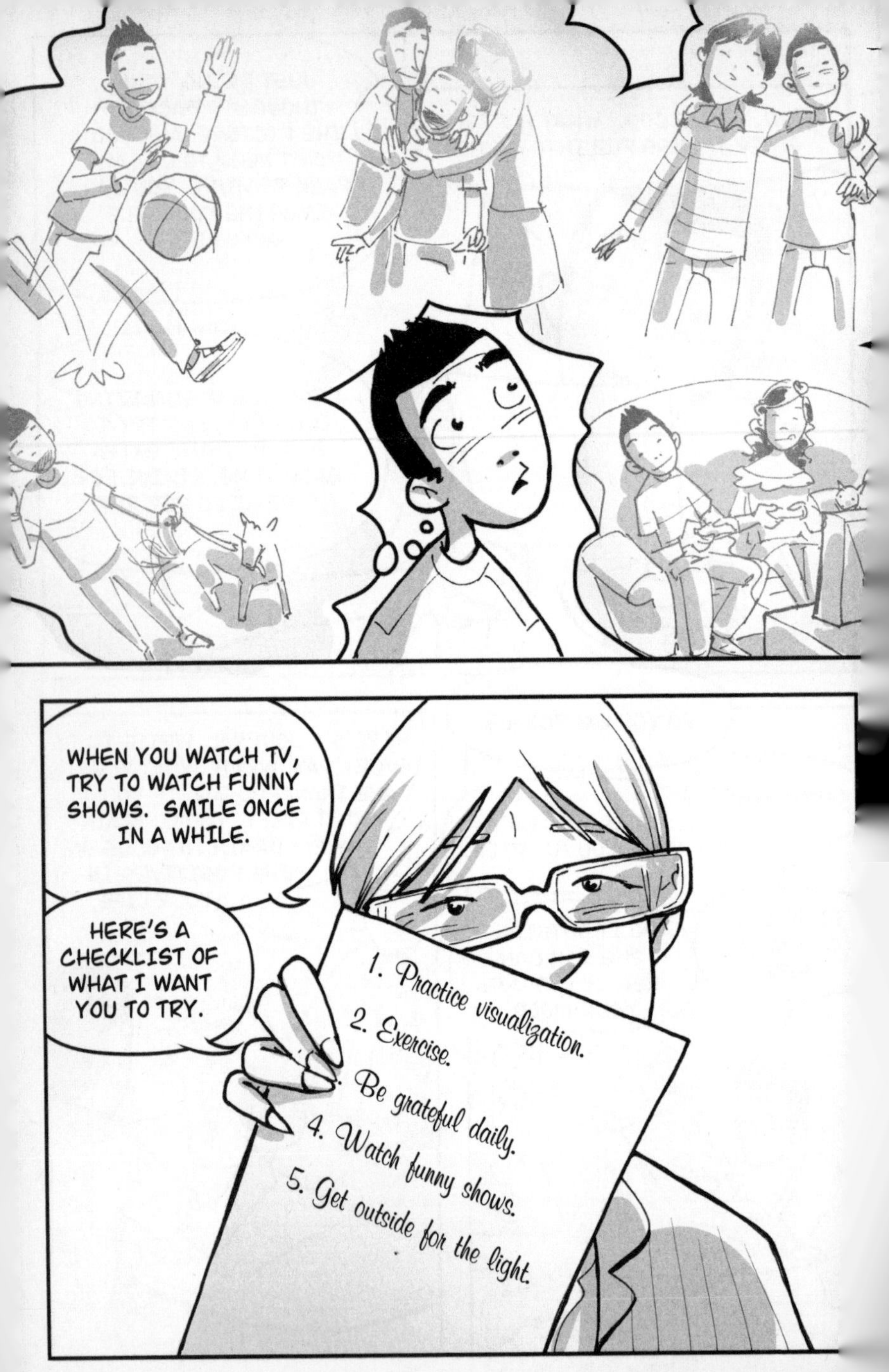
WHEN YOU WATCH TV, TRY TO WATCH FUNNY SHOWS. SMILE ONCE IN A WHILE.
HERE'S A CHECKLIST OF WHAT I WANT YOU TO TRY.
1. Practice visualization.
2. Exercise.
Be grateful daily.
4. Watch funny shows.
5. Get outside for the light.

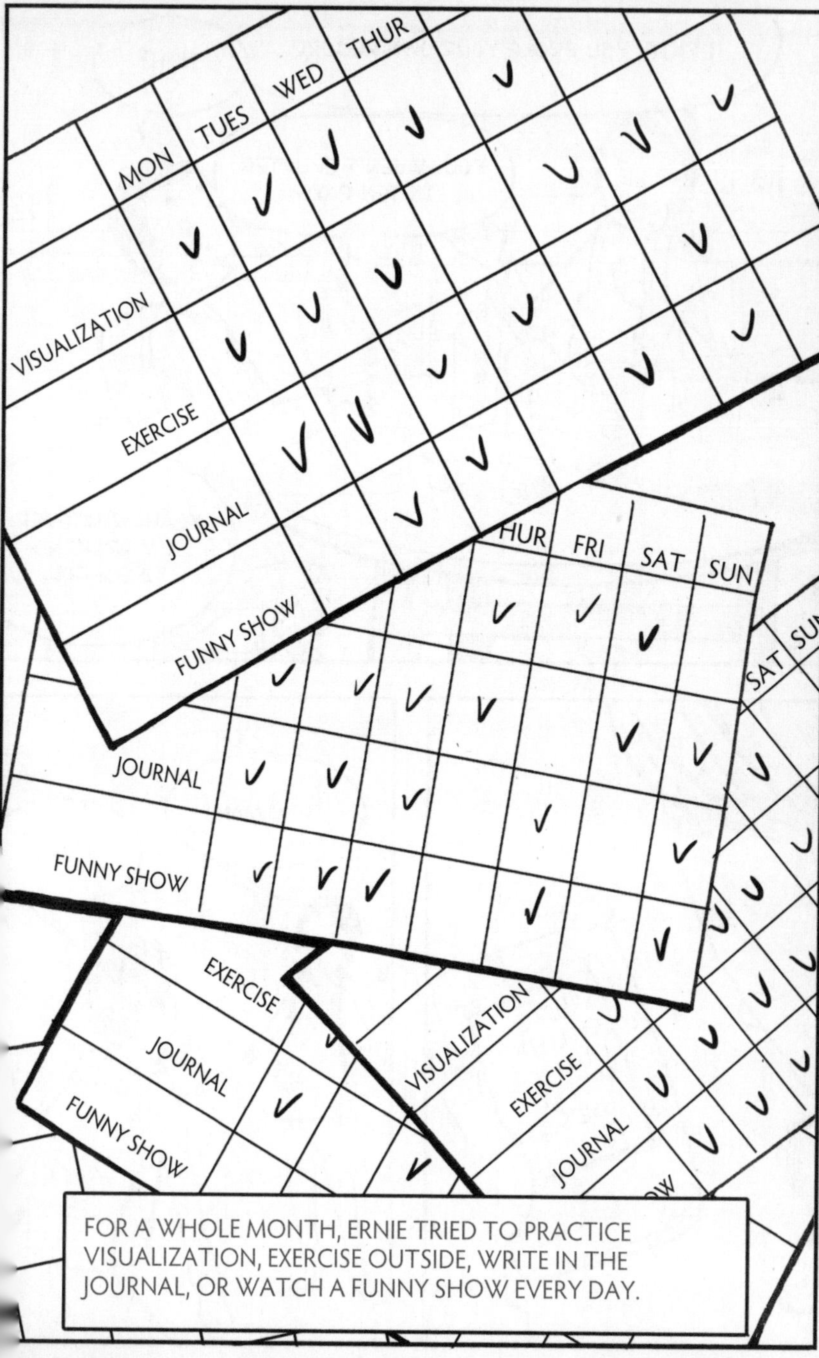
MON
TUES
WED
THUR
VISUALIZATION
EXERCISE
JOURNAL
FUNNY SHOW
HUR
FRI
SAT
SUN
JOURNAL
FUNNY SHOW
SAT
EXERCISE
JOURNAL
FUNNY SHOW
VISUALIZATION
EXERCISE
JOURNAL
FOR A WHOLE MONTH, ERNIE TRIED TO PRACTICE VISUALIZATION, EXERCISE OUTSIDE, WRITE IN THE JOURNAL, OR WATCH A FUNNY SHOW EVERY DAY.

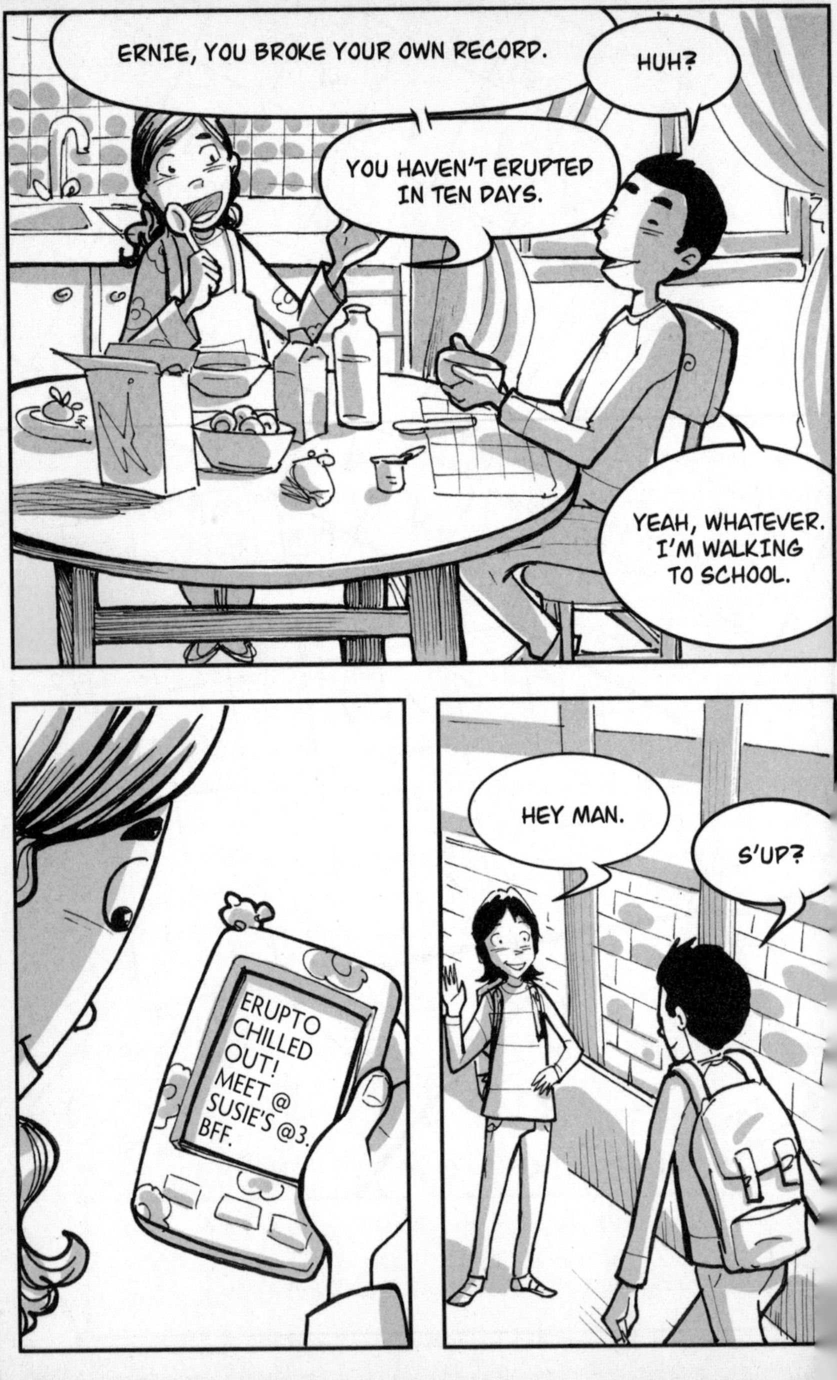
ERNIE, YOU BROKE YOUR OWN RECORD.
HUH?
YOU HAVEN'T ERUPTED IN TEN DAYS.
YEAH, WHATEVER. I'M WALKING TO SCHOOL.
ERUPTO CHILLED OUT! MEET @ SUSIE'S @3. BFF.
HEY MAN.
S'UP?

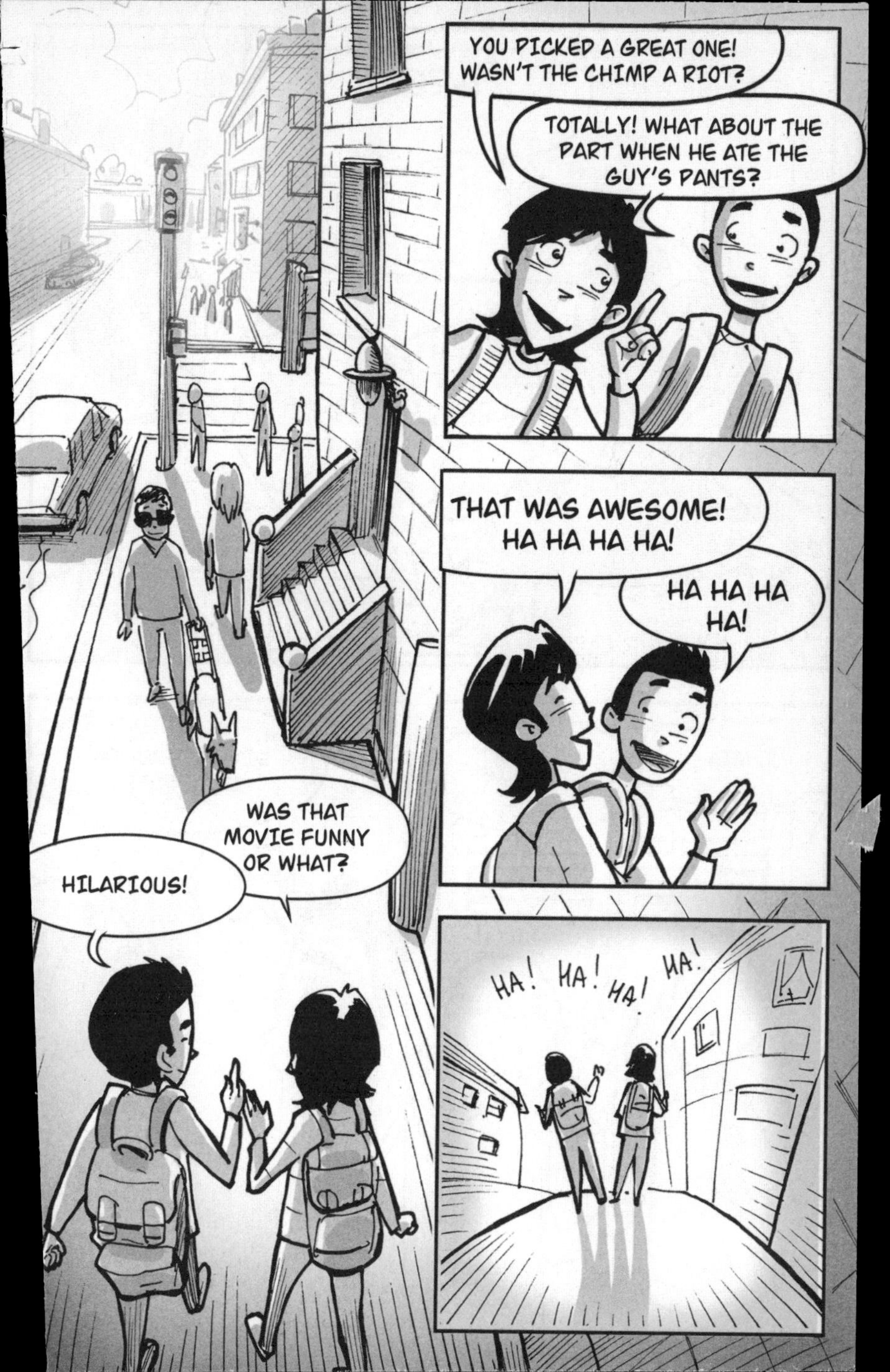
YOU PICKED A GREAT ONE! WASN'T THE CHIMP A RIOT?
TOTALLY! WHAT ABOUT THE PART WHEN HE ATE THE GUY'S PANTS?
THAT WAS AWESOME! HA HA HA HA!
HA HA HA HA!
WAS THAT MOVIE FUNNY OR WHAT?
HILARIOUS!
HA! HA! HA! HA!

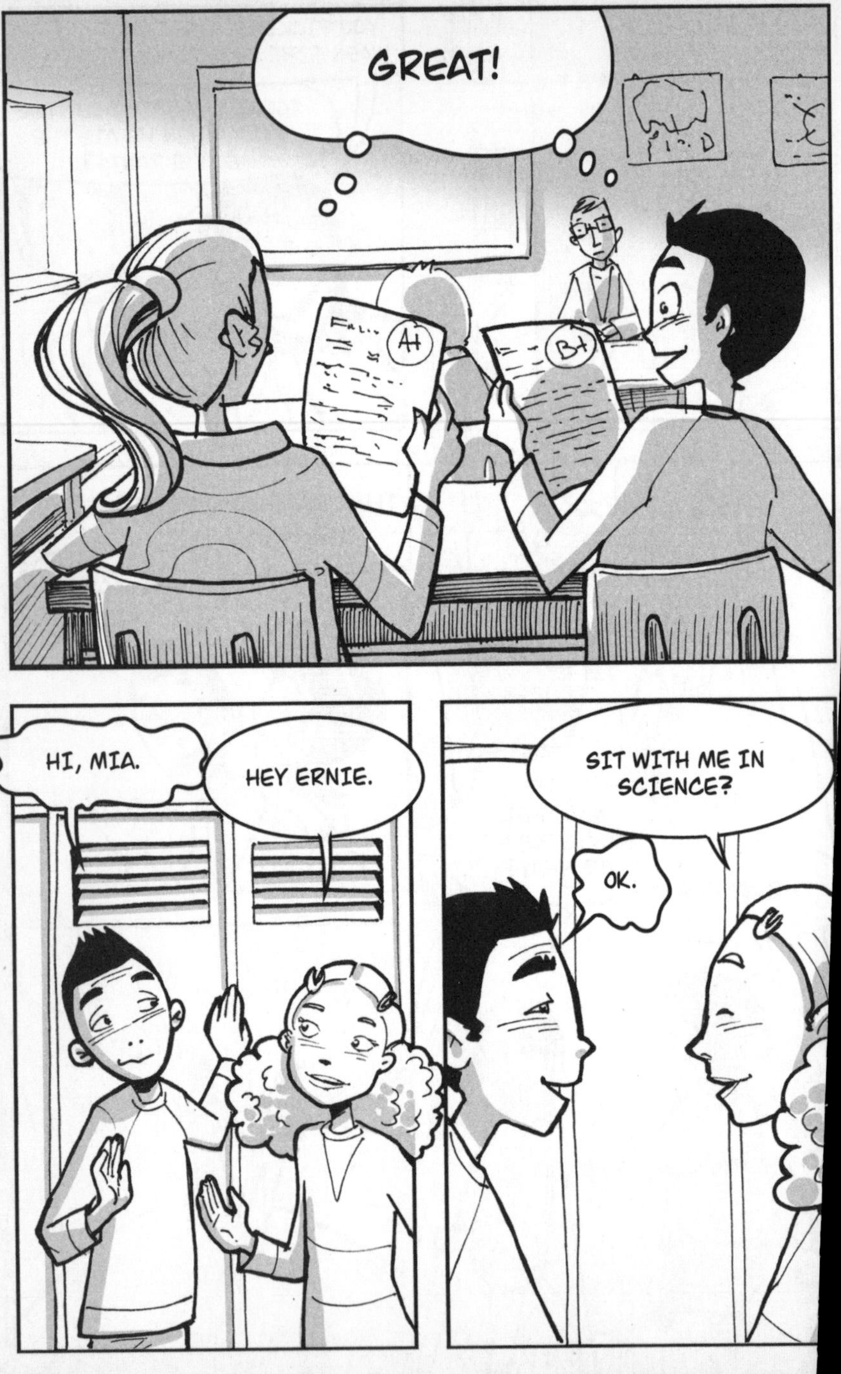
GREAT!
HI, MIA.
HEY ERNIE.
SIT WITH ME IN SCIENCE?
OK.

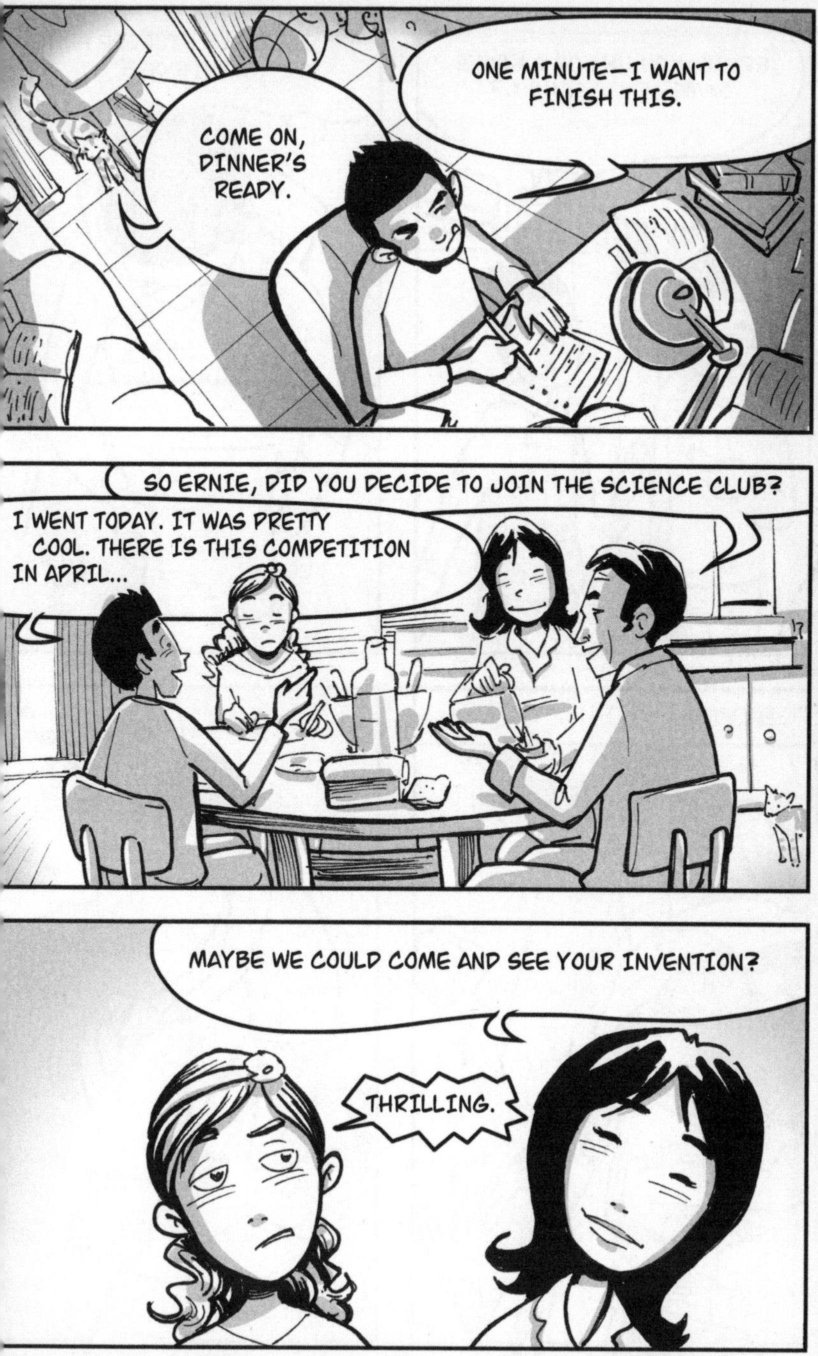
COME ON, DINNER'S READY.
ONE MINUTE—I WANT TO FINISH THIS.
SO ERNIE, DID YOU DECIDE TO JOIN THE SCIENCE CLUB?
I WENT TODAY. IT WAS PRETTY COOL. THERE IS THIS COMPETITION IN APRIL...
MAYBE WE COULD COME AND SEE YOUR INVENTION?
THRILLING.

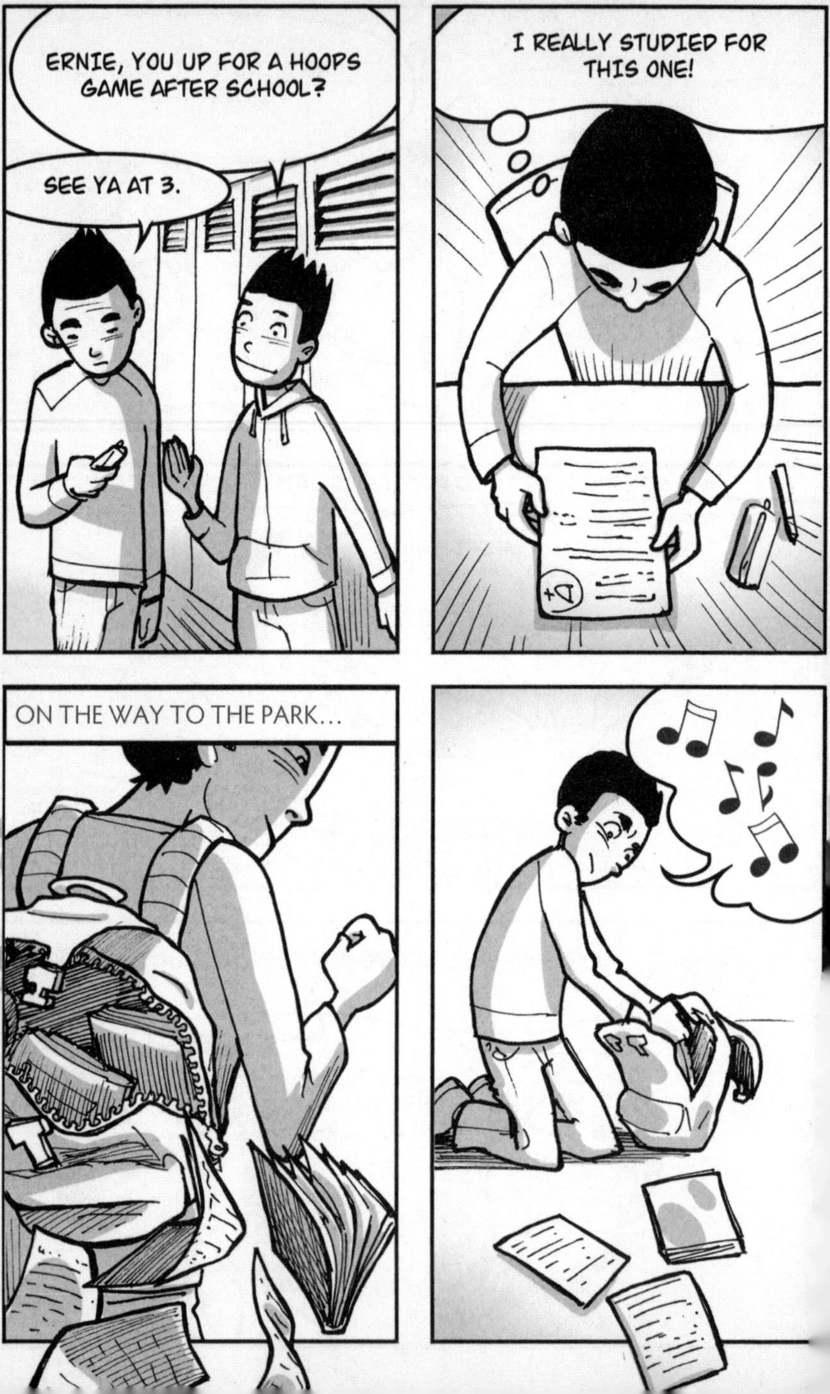
ERNIE, YOU UP FOR A HOOPS GAME AFTER SCHOOL?
SEE YA AT 3.
I REALLY STUDIED FOR THIS ONE!
D+
ON THE WAY TO THE PARK...

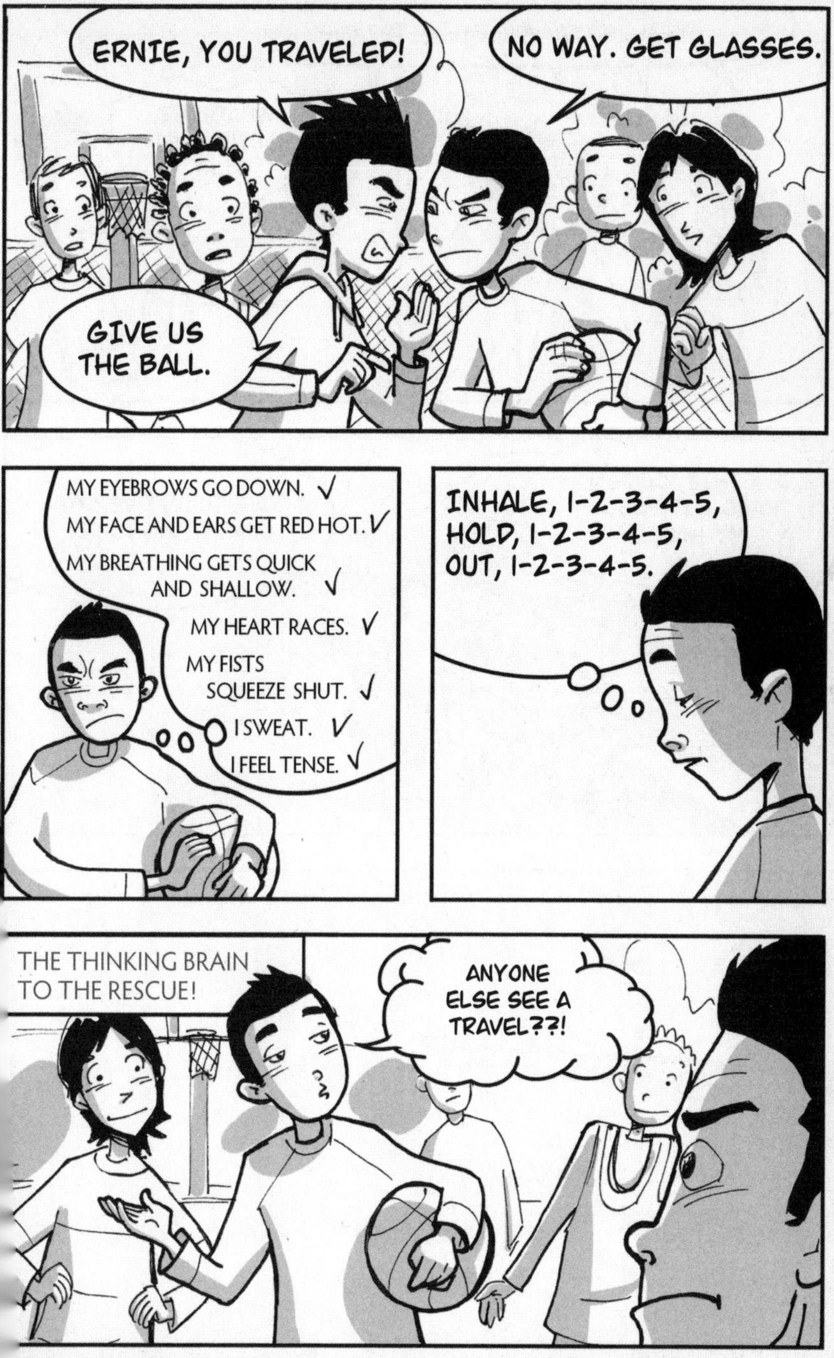
ERNIE, YOU TRAVELED!
NO WAY. GET GLASSES.
GIVE US THE BALL.
MY EYEBROWS GO DOWN. ✓
MY FACE AND EARS GET RED HOT. ✓
MY BREATHING GETS QUICK AND SHALLOW. ✓
MY HEART RACES. ✓
MY FISTS SQUEEZE SHUT. ✓
I SWEAT. ✓
I FEEL TENSE. ✓
INHALE, 1-2-3-4-5,
HOLD, 1-2-3-4-5,
OUT, 1-2-3-4-5.
THE THINKING BRAIN TO THE RESCUE!
ANYONE ELSE SEE A TRAVEL??!

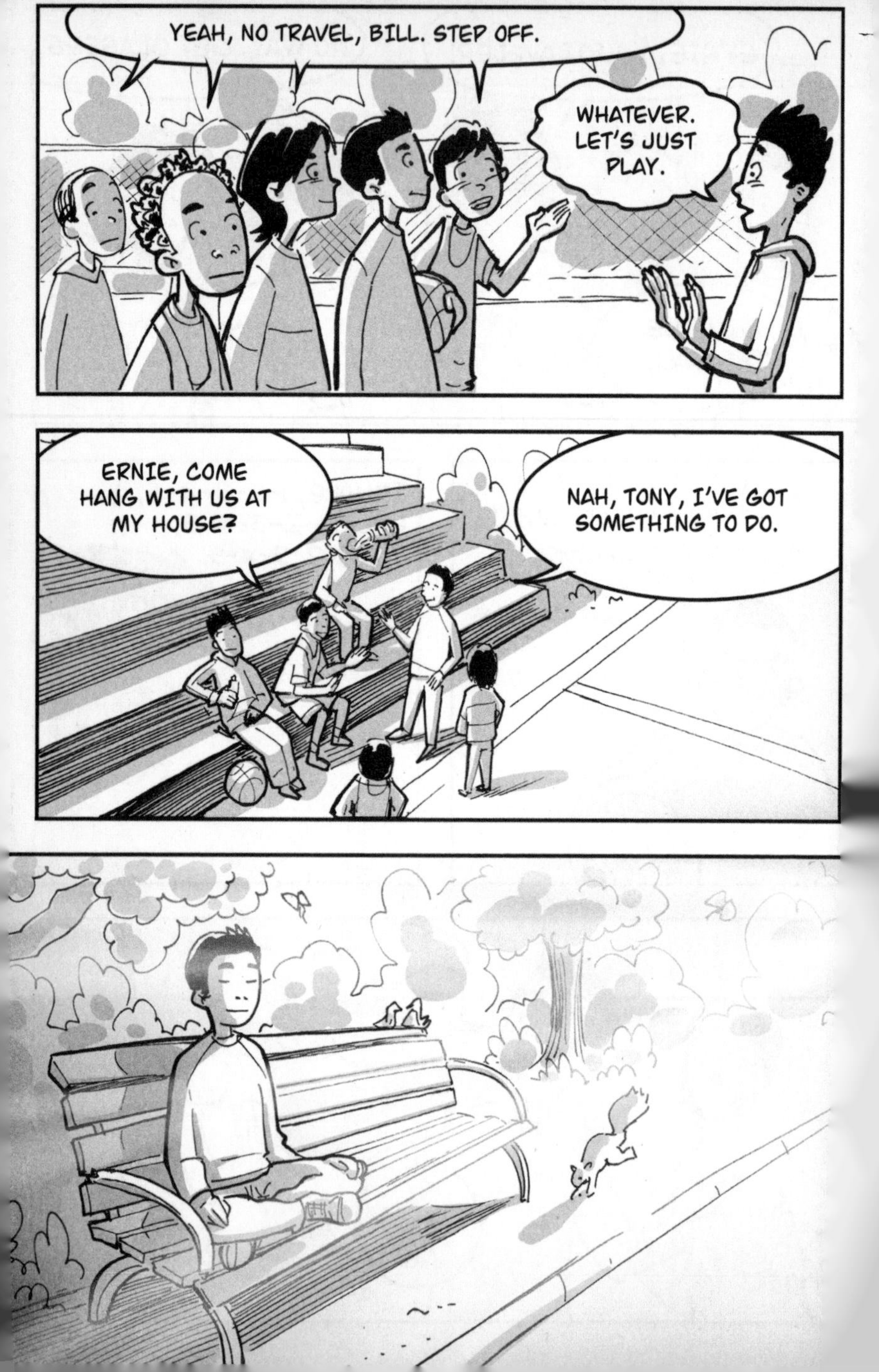
YEAH, NO TRAVEL, BILL. STEP OFF.
WHATEVER. LET'S JUST PLAY.
ERNIE, COME HANG WITH US AT MY HOUSE?
NAH, TONY, I'VE GOT SOMETHING TO DO.

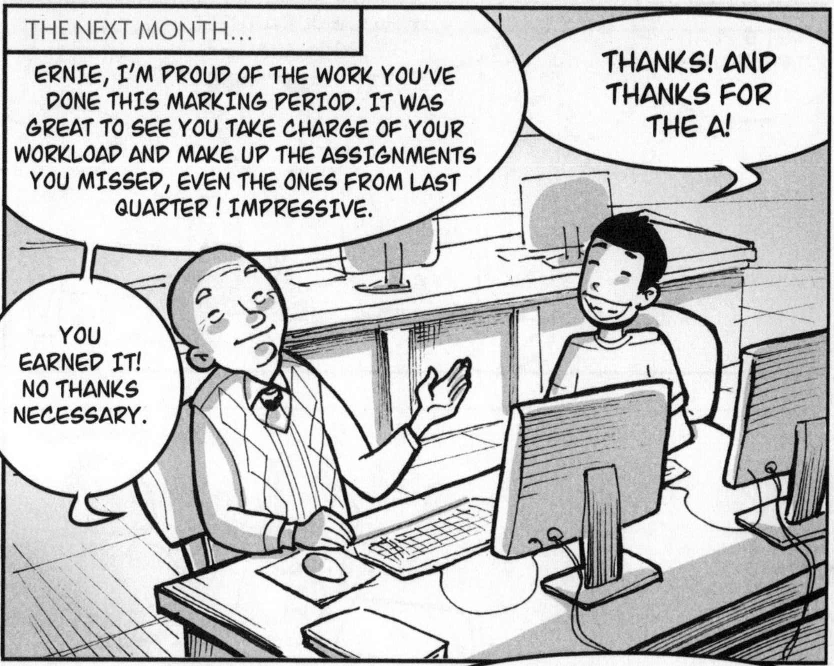
THE NEXT MONTH…
ERNIE, I'M PROUD OF THE WORK YOU'VE DONE THIS MARKING PERIOD. IT WAS GREAT TO SEE YOU TAKE CHARGE OF YOUR WORKLOAD AND MAKE UP THE ASSIGNMENTS YOU MISSED, EVEN THE ONES FROM LAST QUARTER ! IMPRESSIVE.
THANKS! AND THANKS FOR THE A!
YOU EARNED IT! NO THANKS NECESSARY.

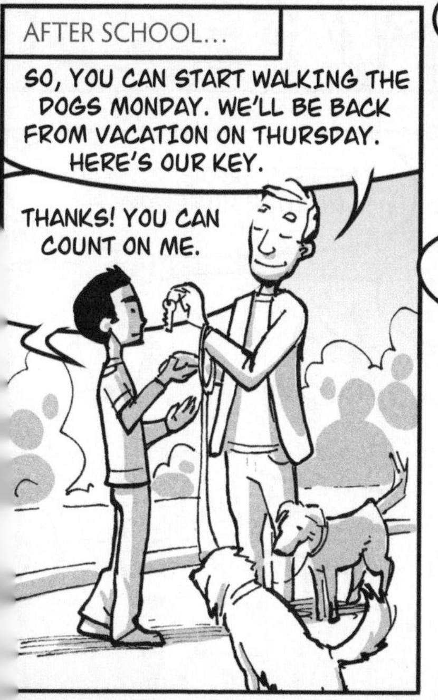
AFTER SCHOOL…
SO, YOU CAN START WALKING THE DOGS MONDAY. WE'LL BE BACK FROM VACATION ON THURSDAY. HERE'S OUR KEY.
THANKS! YOU CAN COUNT ON ME.

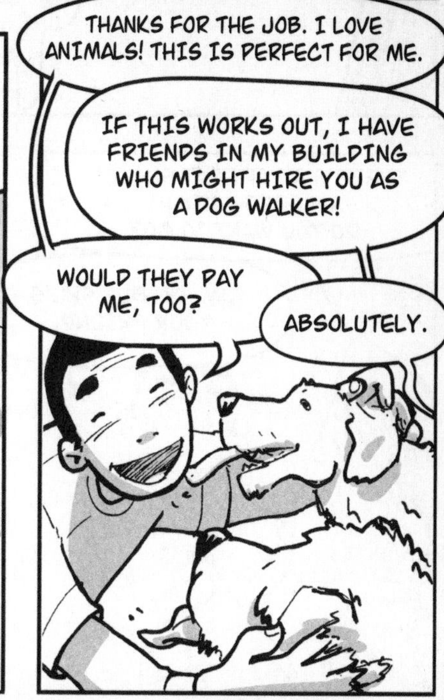
THANKS FOR THE JOB. I LOVE ANIMALS! THIS IS PERFECT FOR ME.
IF THIS WORKS OUT, I HAVE FRIENDS IN MY BUILDING WHO MIGHT HIRE YOU AS A DOG WALKER!
WOULD THEY PAY ME, TOO?
ABSOLUTELY.

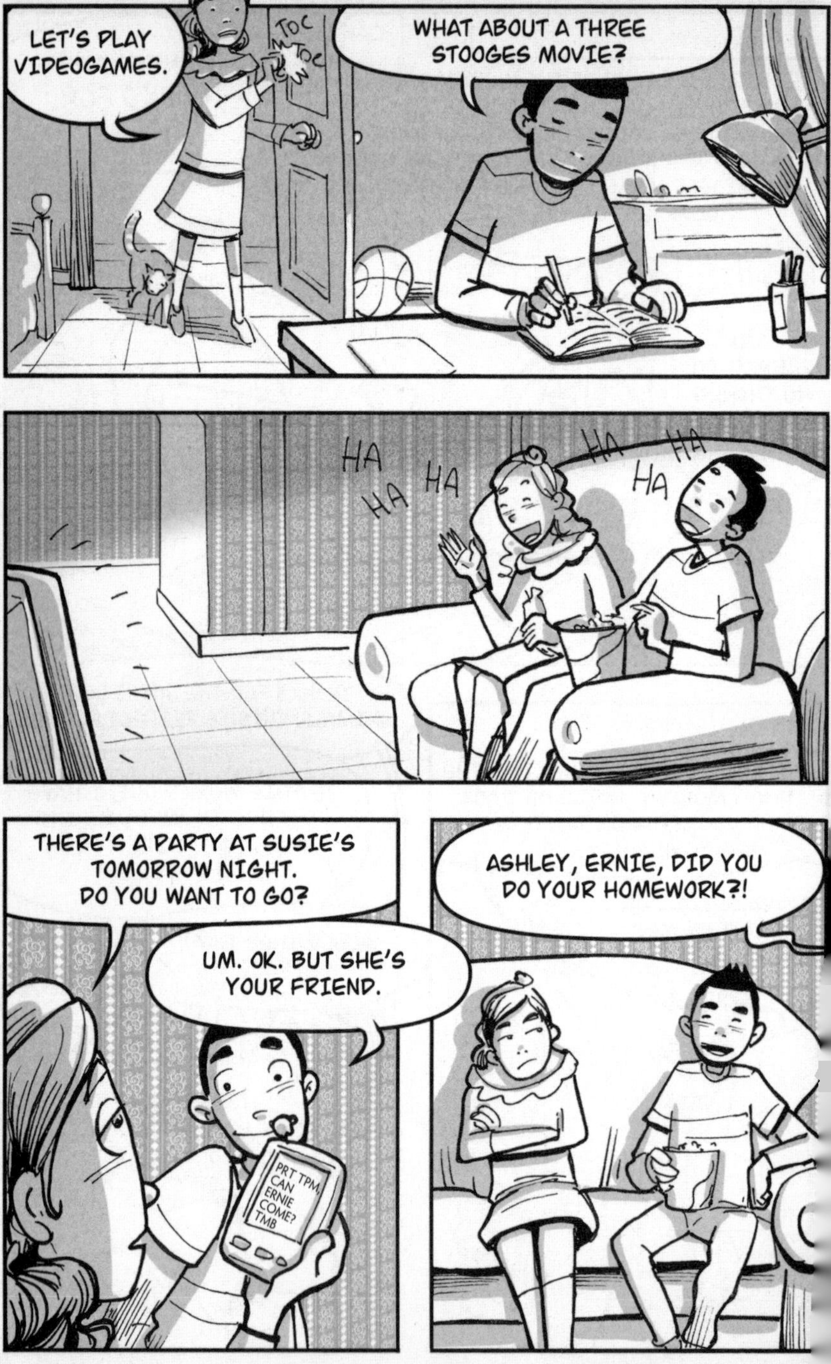
LET'S PLAY VIDEOGAMES.
TOC TOC
WHAT ABOUT A THREE STOOGES MOVIE?
HA HA HA HA HA HA
THERE'S A PARTY AT SUSIE'S TOMORROW NIGHT. DO YOU WANT TO GO?
UM. OK. BUT SHE'S YOUR FRIEND.
PRT TPM, CAN ERNIE COME? TMB
ASHLEY, ERNIE, DID YOU DO YOUR HOMEWORK?!

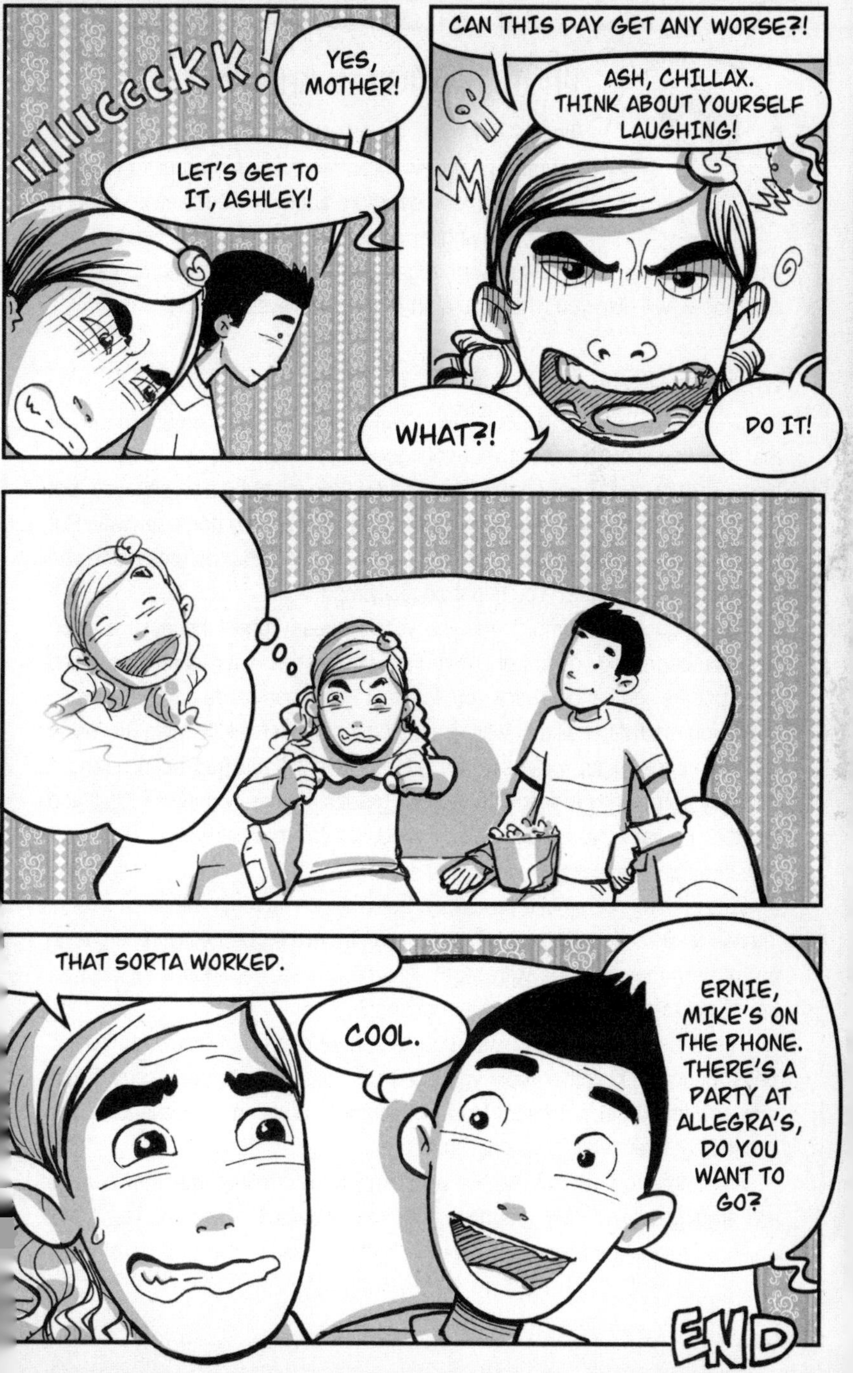

YES, MOTHER!
LET'S GET TO IT, ASHLEY!
CAN THIS DAY GET ANY WORSE?!
ASH, CHILLAX. THINK ABOUT YOURSELF LAUGHING!
WHAT?!
DO IT!
THAT SORTA WORKED.
COOL.
ERNIE, MIKE'S ON THE PHONE. THERE'S A PARTY AT ALLEGRA'S, DO YOU WANT TO GO?
END

Understanding Anger

One of the most important things you can do to take control of anger is to understand it. In order to Chillax!, you'll need to know more about what makes you angry, how being angry makes your body feel, and what you do when you're angry. Knowing about anger, and especially knowing about your own anger, will help you when you start practicing ways to keep it in control.

WHAT MAKES YOU ANGRY?

Imagine you've decided to stay home to watch TV when your parents announce that they need you to babysit your younger sister. Would you be okay with this plan, or really mad at your parents and sister? You might be a bit annoyed, but probably not too upset, because you were planning to stay home anyway. But what if you'd planned to go to a friend's big party and your parents made you stay home and babysit? You might be really mad.

Here's another example: Imagine you're already upset because a good friend embarrassed you in front of your class, and then your teacher assigned three papers and handed back your last test with a bad grade on it. That could make you mad. After all that was already upsetting you, a little thing like losing a board game might really set you off. However, if you had been having a perfectly normal day (no teasing, no bad grades, normal homework load) and lost a board game, you might not be thrilled, but you most likely would not react with strong angry feelings.

Lots of things can make you angry. But why do you react with such strong, intense feelings sometimes? Why can you sometimes be OK with setbacks, and other times explode with rage? How you react depends a lot on your emotional state and what is in your backpack.

The backpack you carry with you to school contains homework, books, pens, pencils, and other tools you need for class. But you also carry "stuff" around with you in a different kind of backpack: emotions, experiences, and events that affect your emotional state.

From time to time, we all have a backpack full of things like: "My parents are arguing again," "My grandma is in the hospital," "I failed a test," "My algebra teacher thinks I'm an idiot," "My friend teased me in front of other kids," "My sister is going to the movies without me," and even, "I'm hungry." If your backpack is empty when a small trigger occurs—let's say someone elbows you in the busy hallway—you may be able to brush it off as an accident or a non-event. But if your emotional backpack is heavy or overflowing with experiences and things that are bothering you, then that little elbow may be enough for you to start a shoving match in the hallway. Strong anger can be triggered by something that tweaks your emotional state and unleashes your feelings in an intense and strong way.

Think about how heavy your backpack is right now. Do you have any ideas about what's really bothering you? What's your emotional state? Sometimes it is not so easy to figure out what you are carrying around emotionally, so you might need to dig deep and think about what is bothering you and think about what you did (or didn't) do when you were angry.

HOW DOES IT FEEL WHEN YOU ARE ANGRY?

What happens when you get angry? How does it show in your body? What does it feel like when you are starting to get angry?

Sometimes, anger can make you feel hot and irritated, other times you may feel heavy and down, and sometimes it can make you feel restless and tight. All these feelings are in your body and are signals that you are angry. No matter how anger makes you feel, using those bodily clues to identify that you are angry is crucial to dealing with this emotion and, eventually, changing how your mind and body react when you are really, really mad.

You may experience different physical signals than someone else and the type and intensity of bodily signals are different for each person. You may need a counselor or parent to help you identify your body's signs, because when you are angry it can be hard to think. But you are in control of your body, so once you know how you feel when you're angry, you can work on creating more appropriate actions.

WHAT DO YOU DO WHEN YOU ARE ANGRY?

Anger can make it hard to think and can cause you to resort to "fight or flight" reflexes. These reflexes tell you to stand your ground and fight against a threat or flee a situation. You might yell or want to run or physically fight back against something that is upsetting you. These reflexes, left over from our caveman ancestors, can be valuable self-protective responses. We need these reflexes to react to dangerous situations.

However, many times it is more appropriate to take another action and leave the caveman responses with the caveman. Some ways of expressing your anger can cause more hurt and embarrassment, or can simply make it all worse, so it's important to develop helpful ways to respond when you're angry. It can take a while to learn that you need to try to calm down and temper your anger and switch on your *thinking brain* before you respond to an emotional trigger.

How To Chillax!

There's a lot you can do to get in control of your brain and your body and learn to react to trigger situations in a helpful way. First, there are some things you can practice to help yourself turn on your thinking brain when you start to feel angry. Also, there are things you can do in your daily life, whether you're feeling angry or not, that can help make you less likely to get angry in the first place.

DEALING WITH ANGER TRIGGERS

There are lots of things you can try to do when you need to temper your anger quickly and turn on your thinking brain. Here are some strategies that can help you calm your anger in the moment and help your thinking brain kick in to solve the problem or choose an appropriate action. Remember, you may feel as if you can't think when you feel angry, so you'll need to practice these strategies until they are automatic. That way, you won't need much thinking.

S = SING A SONG
W = WALK AWAY
I = IMAGINE YOURSELF LAUGHING
F = FAKE A SMILE
T = TAKE COVER
B = BREATHE

Sing a Song. Music changes mood. In a survey that asked teens to name how they feel when listening to music, common responses were: calm, exhilarated, inspired, joyful, carefree, and happy. How do you feel when you listen to music? Something about our favorite song and its meaningful lyrics transports and transforms us. Hum, sing, or even think about your favorite song during stressful moments to give yourself an opportunity to cool off and see the situation differently. With your new perspective, you can rethink what happened, how you arrived at the stressful moment, and what you will do next.

Walk Away. Walking away from a maddening situation empowers you to gain control and choose an intelligent course of action. When you walk away, you give yourself an opportunity to take a time-out from a situation and create physical as well as an emotional or mental distance from the situation. However, don't walk yourself into something dangerous, or storm off somewhere that will make the situation worse. Storming away from a parent when they're your ride home doesn't tend to help things!

Imagine Yourself Laughing. This technique will be most helpful if you practice it before you really need it. You'll need concentration and the ability to remove yourself mentally from the situation you are in and place yourself in a previous, happier situation. Some people find that closing their eyes improves their focus; others work on imagining a complete scene from when they laughed, thinking about where they were and who they were with to vividly recreate a moment in time.

Fake a Smile. Physiologically, faking a smile slows blood flow to the brain, which is exactly what you need to combat the extra blood your increased heart rate is pumping to it when you feel angry. Faking a smile can negate one of the physical signs of anger. Researchers found that if you create the typical facial expression that people make when they are happy—in other words, smile or grin or laugh—you can actually feel that emotion. You can feel happy! And, when you fake a smile, you will become more able to eventually want to smile for real. Try this: Label how you feel, and now try to grin and hold it for 15 seconds. How do you feel now?

Take Cover. When you're feeling angry, it's OK to simply say, "I need a minute," "Hold on," or, "Stop." Taking cover can keep you from becoming too angry. By asking for a break, you can stop everything—your negative thoughts, the momentum of whatever is occurring, any judgments you're passing about people, and anything else that is negatively affecting your emotions. Life moves fast and taking a minute to pause the action can help you regain your composure and give you time to think. You can then move to one of the other SWIFT-B strategies, but you might also find that taking cover alone will put you back in control of your feelings and, consequently, the situation.

Breathe. Breathing techniques are great for combatting the rapid, shallow breathing that often accompanies anger. Breathing calms our body and our behavioral responses to anger. Here's how you do it: Begin by breathing in for a count of five, then holding for a count of five, followed by exhaling for five. Repeat this pattern until you feel calm. This repetition turns out-of-control breathing into a structured bodily response. It also provides a distraction from the situation that is making you mad. By focusing on breathing, the trigger situation becomes secondary and you can put it into perspective. Practice this controlled breathing before you need it. That will make this calming method more effective.

UNLOADING YOUR EMOTIONAL LOAD

In addition to dealing with your bodily response to anger while you're feeling angry, you can do things to calm your mind and emotions, which will help you react more appropriately when something triggers your anger. You can practice breathing, visualization, and other things like exercise, laughter, gratefulness, and communication to reduce anger. These tools work to empty your backpack and lighten your emotional load, improving your overall mood.

Visualization. To accomplish visualization, focus on a picture. Find a picture of something in nature or any calming scene. Sit in a comfortable position and focus your attention on that picture. Look at the details and notice the colors, the shades, the shapes, and anything else about it you see. If upsetting or unrelated thoughts inundate you, let them flow past you while you continue to concentrate on the picture.

Here's how to do it:
1. Think of a calm scene in a picture or a place you know.
2. Focus on the picture, or close your eyes and imagine the familiar place in your mind.
3. Explore that place using all your senses—what do you hear? Smell? See? Feel?

4. Begin to notice how your body feels. Are you relaxed? Quiet? Calm?

5. Continue to look at the picture or imagine the familiar place until you are completely at ease.

When you finish visualizing, slowly open your eyes and notice how your body feels when it's in a relaxed state. Focus on your shoulders, your jaw, your hands, and your face. How do they feel when they're relaxed, compared to when you're in an angry state? Noticing these differences will help you identify the initial signs of anger. Visualization requires practice.

Exercise. Just as there are mental health benefits to meditating, there are benefits to exercising. Exercise improves mood, alleviates stress, calms nerves, and increases self-esteem. Like meditation and visualization, exercise requires that you focus your energy on the activity you're performing in the moment. The time you spend focusing on having fun and being active can distract you from your unhelpful thoughts.

Find an exercise that suits you. How about running? Taking a dance class? Sledding? Taking a walk in the woods? Even simply walking up flights of steps qualifies. Try to exercise outside in the sunshine because natural light improves mood, too.

Laughter. Another way to increase good feelings is through laughter. There's a reason people say that laughter is the best medicine. But how often do you laugh? For most of us the answer is, "not enough." Make time to watch funny TV shows. If you don't know of any, ask an adult or do a search online. Remember, just like faking a smile, laughter makes more laughter and it will improve your overall mood.

Gratefulness. Another simple strategy to improve our outlook is to engage in grateful behavior. Sometimes we forget to take time and be thankful for what we have, because we are so focused on what we don't have. When was the last time you thought, "Wow, I am so thankful that I have a cell phone"? Most likely you've thought of the new phone you want, or the one your friend just received. Taking the time to be thankful in a purposeful way, by writing down what you're grateful for or talking in detail about it with someone you trust, can improve your mood. You might be thankful for obvious things, like great friends or your new puppy, but there are endless opportunities to be grateful if you think about often-unnoticed things like snowflakes, gummy candy, the smell of cut grass, the start of baseball season, a sunny day, music, a day without homework, a hug, a helpful teacher, or a favorite pair of jeans. Fill a book with all of them, and you might be surprised by what you can come up with!

Communication. One important strategy for controlling anger is communication. It can feel too embarrassing to talk about your anger with parents, friends, or a counselor, but holding your feelings in makes you isolated. Over time, it can be easy to think you're the only person with so much anger. Talking about anger can help you realize that you are not alone. When you discuss your feelings with someone you trust, you are emptying your backpack.

One way to practice empowering communication is to use "I statements." I statements allow you to express what you are feeling, and using them can alert the person you're talking to that his or her behavior needs to change. It sounds like this: "I feel_____ when you _____. I need you to _____." So, if you have a friend who is making you angry, you might say something like, "Jack, I feel annoyed when you act like you know everything. I need you to chill on the attitude." By using this assertive, but not aggressive, communication you can address behaviors that are bothering you without getting overly angry.

The delivery, tone, and body language you use when you're making your I statements count, too. Try this: look at the floor and say in a high-pitched, soft voice, "I feel angry when you laugh at me. I need you to stop." Not too convincing? Now say it in a deeper voice, with good eye contact, and standing in a strong position (your hands on your hips or crossed in front of you like a judge): "I feel angry when you laugh at me and I need you to stop." Practice it in front of a mirror so that when you need to use an I statement, you can do it in a way that makes you feel like you have control.

You might be thinking that, while it sounds like a good idea to assertively declare your feelings in an I statement, you might not be ready for it just yet. That's OK. A good first step is to begin a journal. Take a notebook or staple a few pages together and write or draw about your feelings, your experiences, or your relationships. No one needs to see it except you, so keep it in a safe place, and do not bring it to school. Writing or drawing about your feelings is like taking your emotions out of your backpack and putting them onto the paper, and it can help relieve you of your negative mood.

Remember, you want to combat that feeling of isolation, so push yourself to share or set a goal to share, even if you're only sharing with a piece of paper for now. By communicating your feelings and emotions, you are unpacking things from your emotional backpack, and hopefully realizing that other people have dealt with and overcome a lot of the struggles you're facing.

Resources

SELECTED BIBLIOGRAPHY

These are books and articles that support some of the ideas in the book about becoming more contented.

- Achor, S. (2010). *The happiness advantage: The seven principles of positive psychology that fuel success and performance at work.* New York: Crown Business.

- Ekman, P. (1993). Facial expression and emotion. *American Psychologist*, 48, 384–392.

- Emmons, R. (2008). *Thanks! How practicing gratitude can make you happier.* New York: First Houghton Mifflin.

- Zajonc, R.B., Murphy, S.T., & Inglehart, M. (1989). Feeling and facial efference: Implications of the vascular theory of emotions. *Psychological Review*, 96, 395–416.

ADDITIONAL RESOURCES

Listed below are books and articles that may be helpful — some relate to anger management while others are about specific emotions and feelings.

- Ben-Shahar, T. (2007). *Happier: Learn the secrets to daily joy and lasting fulfillment.* New York: McGraw-Hill.

- Crist, J. J. (2008). *Mad: How to deal with your anger and get respect.* Minneapolis, MN: Free Spirit.

- Hipp, E. (2008). *Fighting invisible tigers: Stress management for teens* (3rd ed). Minneapolis, MN: Free Spirit.

- Lamia, M.C. (2011). *Understanding myself: A kid's guide to intense emotions and strong feelings.* Washington, DC: American Psychological Association.

- Lyubomirsky, S. (2007). *The how of happiness: A scientific approach to getting the life you want.* New York: Penguin Press.

- Tompkins, M. A., Martinez, K. (2010). *My anxious mind: A teen's guide to managing anxiety and panic.* Washington, DC: American Psychological Association.

About the Author

MARCELLA MARINO CRAVER, MSED, CAS, has practiced School Psychology in public schools in New York and New Jersey for seventeen years. She is the author of *Learn to Study: A Comprehensive Guide to Academic Success* and gives student and parent presentations on effective and efficient study strategies. She lives with her wonderful husband, their two musically inclined teenagers, and a mischievous cat, who all fill her life with love, music, and laughter.

About the Illustrator

AMERIGO PINELLI lives in the heart of Naples, among narrow streets and churches. A long time ago, when he was a child, he met a pencil, and from that moment on he started to play, joke, fight, and make peace with it. He dreams of becoming a cartoon character...but some say that he already is. You can find him chasing pigeons on the roof when the sun climbs on the Vesuvio. Just ask his wife, Giulia.

About Magination Press

MAGINATION PRESS publishes self-help books for kids and the adults in their lives. Magination Press in an imprint of the American Psychological Association, the largest scientific and professional organization representing psychologists in the United States and the largest association of psychologists worldwide.